P9-CQE-530

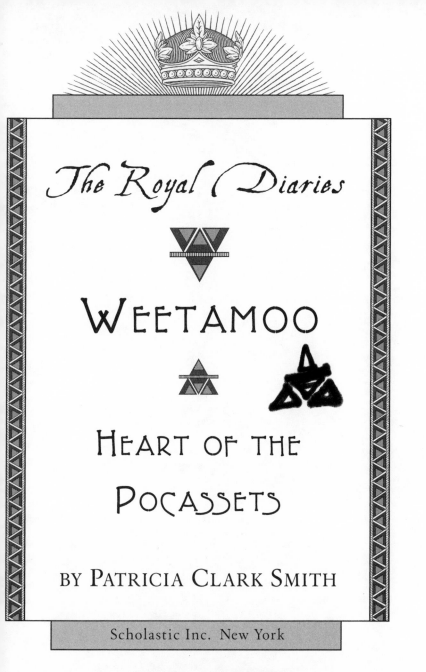

The Royal Diaries

WEETAMOO

HEART OF THE
POCASSETS

BY PATRICIA CLARK SMITH

Scholastic Inc. New York

Pacetti Bay Middle School

Foreword

Weetamoo is a unique subject in The Royal Diaries series. Unlike other young women of the series, Weetamoo did not read or write, and would not have kept a diary in the traditional sense of written accounts of her daily life. Weetamoo's Wampanoag people had many other ways of recording things important to them. They etched pictures on rock, drew on birch bark, and wove coded messages into the intricate patterns of wampum belts made of white and purple clamshell beads. Above all, they were an oral culture. The Wampanoags' ability to listen carefully and remember well was prodigious. By word of mouth, they passed down stories and histories, genealogies, prayers, recipes, ceremonies, ways of healing, and all that told them who they were and how to survive.

As this book suggests, Native Americans of the seventeenth century in Massachusetts understood the potential power and usefulness of English writing. But the only

Indians admitted to English schools were those who were willing to accept Christianity and English ways of life. Weetamoo was not one of those. And so to present the story of this brilliant Native American woman leader in her girlhood, we have imagined here what her thoughts and experiences might have been, and how she might have kept track of them.

We hope some sense of the wisdom of her people is conveyed in this fictional account of the real Weetamoo.

MASSACHUSETTS—
RHODE ISLAND,
1653

NEEPUNNA KEESWUSH
MOON WHEN CORN IS RIPE
[LATE AUGUST 1653]
METTAPOISET

I am Weetamoo, daughter of Corbitant, sachem over the Pocasset band of our Wampanoag Nation. It is about to be my fourteenth winter, and I am sitting here on a hollow log atop this hill.

As Father and Mother have bidden me, I am thinking and praying to Squant, the Being who watches over us girls and women.

To tell the truth, I would rather be clamming.

Never mind, though . . . here is my prayer:

Please, Squant, grant me patience.

But I was tempted to ask Father if when he and Mother were young, or even all the way back when the world was new, whether children weren't sometimes as restless as I? Wouldn't they rather have been laughing with their friends and digging their toes into the wet muck on the tide flats, pulling up fat, juicy quahogs for supper, instead of sitting still and hoping for someone to help them become patient?

The elders say Squant lingers near us still out on the sand dunes and among the rocky places that line the bay. I wonder if she can hear me?

This is what happened yesterday. Father told me to come walking with him on this same rise that overlooks our seaside village of Mettapoiset. Down below on the sandy shore, I spied the other girls drying fish on the wooden racks set over banked fires, and I was glad to be spared that smoky chore for the moment. I love to hunt for food, and I love to eat it, but I do not much love to prepare it.

I could see clear over the choppy blue waters of the bay all the way to Montaup, where Ousamequin, Yellow Feather, he whom the English Coat-men call Massasoit, often makes his own summer home. He is a great sachem among all the bands of our Wampanoag Nation. He and my father Corbitant have often disagreed in the past about Massasoit's willingness to help these English who call themselves Saints and Pilgrims, these Wautaconuoag pink-faced Coat-men from across the sea whom my father despises. Massasoit says cautiously there may be room for all and thinks it best that we try to get along, but Father distrusts them deeply.

Everyone remembers how when the strangers first came here, they avowed themselves our devoted friends. My father met one Coat-man named Winslow who said to him, "Where true love is, there is no fear." But my father then asked him why, when we visit their Coat-man village, their firearms are always at the ready, and why do they always shoot them into the air, as though to impress us with their might? Winslow said this salute was meant to honor us as guests, but my father said, "I like not such salutations!"

My father loves to laugh and joke, but he is also the most serious person I know. He and Massasoit get on well enough now, but I think they will always disagree about the Coat-men.

I was pointing out to Father how a few trees might be just beginning to turn yellow over there to the west on Massasoit's peninsula of Montaup. He nodded, but I could see he did not wish to discuss Massasoit or the change of seasons. Instead, he laid his hand gently on my shoulder and told me that if I, Weetamoo, am to become sachem of us Pocassets after him, and prove a good leader, I must learn to walk more carefully through the world.

I shook my long hair out of my eyes and stared up at him in surprise. I said he surely could not mean that I was poor at tracking game or at passing unseen through the woods. He knows I can follow almost any trail, and he has seen for himself how I can edge my way near enough to a doe and her pair of speckled fawns to hear their three separate breaths. Did he not teach me all these skills himself, I spluttered, and was I not better at it than any boy or girl in our village?

Father just looked at me with one eyebrow raised. His silence can be terrible. My voice simply trailed off. I hung my head and looked down at his moccasins, the moccasins I sewed for him. In truth, I thought I knew what he was going to say. After all, I admitted to myself, Father may have taught me well how to stalk and skulk. But he probably does not like the mischievous way I have taken to sneaking up close behind my little sister Wootonekanuske while she is gathering wood or berries so I can jump up and yell PAH! right behind her. I suppose I am sorry for the many times I have gotten her small brown eyes to go big with fright. But she is such a good, quiet girl, sometimes I cannot resist giving her a little scare when I catch her in the woods going so solemnly about her tasks.

After a long minute Father raised my chin with two fingers and made me look at him. He said it was not in the skulking or stalking kind of careful walking that I need improvement. He said I often act too quickly, and thus foolishly, and he said I am far too quick to anger. Moreover, he said, since it was about to be my fourteenth winter, it was time to work on these matters. Then at last he smiled and said he had something he wanted me to do. I feared it would be extra chores, but it was not. Here is what it is.

Father bids me only to sit silently apart from the others for a few minutes each day, and think over all that I have done and said, and what has happened. And he tells me that Mother says I am to pray to Squant, a good Woman Being, for patience.

Thus I sit here again today on the hill overlooking the bay, doing just as Father and Mother ask!

LATER THIS DAY

I have decided I will do something else, too, besides the thinking and the praying, because I am not doing very well as yet with this matter of patience. To sit quietly and wait for a trout to rise to the surface of a pool, or to sit quietly and listen to the stories about Squant and her giant husband, Maushop, and his billows of pipe smoke that cause the fog along the shore — these things I can do easily. But <u>only</u> to sit?

So I have a plan. I have gathered myself a nice big sheaf of clean birchbark, and on it I shall at times make a picture of some one thing that will help me remember what a given day has brought. I can make such pictures with a sharp stick blackened in the fire, and then I put a little deer tallow on my thumb and rub it over the marks to make the charcoal stain deeper. I can hide the birchbark in the blackberry tangle up here on the hill.

Here is my first picture. It is a picture of me drawing a picture.

This is enough thinking for one day!

LATER THAT NIGHT

I do not have my birchbark here. It is back up on the hill under the blackberry bushes. But I am lying here quietly between my dear Auntie White Frost, my mother's sister, and my sister Wootonekanuske, and I am thinking.

I would say it counts as being alone if I am the only one lying awake in my family's *wetu* while everyone else is asleep and snoring.

After Mother caught me quarreling with my sister earlier this evening over whose turn it was to grind corn, she took me aside and reminded me about my name. Weetamoo means Sweet Heart, and my family named me thus so I might bring harmony to our family and our people, she said. I nodded. I expected this. I have heard something of the sort said often, whenever I am present at feasts for babies' naming ceremonies and all the elders sit around and make long speeches on the importance of names.

I know I have a quick temper. But how can I ever learn to be as patient as someone like Mother, when I have such a poky little sister, and when my parents insist I learn to do all the poky tasks children must do?

I am trying because I know it is important, but maybe I will always be the one who complains.

Maybe I will never be the sweet heart of anybody's home.

I just realized I forgot to ask Squant to grant me patience yesterday. So I shall ask it doubly today.

Please, Squant, grant me patience.
Please, Squant, grant me patience.

There.

This morning I got no more than halfway up the hill on my way to find my birchbark at my Sitting-Down-to-Think place before I heard Mother calling me to come help in the cornfield. Now I am back.

If life were only all wading in the tidal river by our seaside village here at Mettapoiset and catching crabs and running races, all tracking deer and snaring rabbits when we are back inland at Nemasket, and being the leader in all things, I think I could be happy and good all the time. But some days how I dislike the endless hoeing and weeding of our fields, and the ordinary kind of sewing that is always waiting for me! I tell you, if I never tan another hide again I shall not be sorry.

And yet, I have to say harvesting the green corn as my mother bid me to do all morning is not the worst chore a person could be given. I always like to remember how our

Mother Corn came to us. I love to hear the story of how the crows, our brave relatives, flew up here from far away to the southwest, carrying the kernels in their beaks, and gave them to us. That is why we never kill these birds. We only scare them away from our fields, and always leave ears of corn behind for them, so they can dine, too.

Today, while we were harvesting, I thought of how much those ripe ears with their silky brown hair look like women. There they hide in their green rustly skirts, and when I snap them gently off the stalk, I love to smell the milky sap on my fingers.

Roast corn tonight! And soon, the big harvest feast, the autumn thanksgiving time. Of course we give thanks around the year — for the fish runs, for the strawberries when they come ripe. But the harvest feast is my favorite.

Here is a picture of Mother Corn:

MICHEENNEE KEESWOSH
TIME OF EVERLASTING FLIES
[EARLY SEPTEMBER]

Tomorrow we will travel across the bay to Montaup, Massasoit's village, for a great green-corn harvest gathering and a parlay that will last for seven days. There will be such food, and at night the big council fires, and storytelling and dancing, and a chance to see the children from other villages, like my friend Cedar. When Cedar is grown, they say she will be sachem of her people, whose seaside village lies just down the point from our Mettapoiset. So one day we think we shall be neighboring women sachems.

We whisper to each other that when she and I are sachems together we will try to govern well and wisely.

Some of our elders say it is near Cedar's village where Squant still dwells. They say she can sometimes be seen wandering out on the shoreline among the big rocks, or that she lies there changed into a rock herself.

If she really is a rock now, as some say, I suppose she must be very patient indeed.

Or is she perhaps sometimes impatient herself, and tired of being a rock?

I am asking Squant to grant me patience, but all the same I cannot wait to see my friend Cedar!

Then there is Massasoit's daughter, Amie, and her big brothers, Wamsutta and Metacom. Amie is not like me and Cedar. She is not very bold, yet she is brave, unlike my sister, and she does not cry when we tease her.

As for those brothers of hers, Metacom, the younger, is so quiet, I do not know him very well. Wamsutta, a little older than me, is quite brave, and says just what he thinks, which I hear sometimes gets him in trouble. He is going to be sachem after Massasoit.

Even though I am a girl, I think perhaps I am something like Wamsutta.

I fear I cannot take my birchbark with me over the water to Montaup, and so it must lie here in its hiding place under the blackberries. Also I do not know if I will be able to find a quiet Thinking Place when we are visitors in a strange village. But I shall remember all that happens, and I shall make pictures somehow when I am there. For now, here is a picture of our dugout canoes:

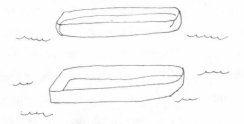

I have slipped away to a rocky point a little north of the encampment to do my thinking. Massasoit's Montaup is a large village. And now there comes a great gathering of many different bands of Wampanoag people, who are bustling all about. I must keep my eyes and ears open to all that is going on.

I want to remember our voyage over here, for a strange thing happened. Not very great, perhaps, but it was a wonder to me.

We crossed the bay this morning, twenty of my family and our relatives in our big dugout, and more dugouts full of other Pocasset families. Mother held our baby sister Snowbird on her lap in the cradleboard and sat toward the stern. Auntie White Frost was seated there, too, busy trying to keep her lively twins, Seal Boy and Gull Girl, from launching themselves overboard. They are going to be two winters old this year, and they are very excitable and wriggly! Wootonekanuske and I helped Auntie for a while, until the motion of the boat lulled both little ones to sleep.

I moved carefully forward then, closer to the paddlers, and watched them at their work. I was thinking I would dearly love to try my own hand at being one of the crew for a seagoing dugout this large. Of course Father has taught me and Wootonekanuske how to paddle small dugouts on the calm waters of our ponds and coves, but manning a giant hollowed-out log of white pine over the whitecaps of the bay seems much more exciting. An ocean life for me!

Because I had nothing much to do on the rest of the voyage over except to hang on and ride, I grew drowsy in the salt spray and hot early autumn sunlight, watching the way the water swirled around the thrusting paddles. Suddenly I saw in my mind's eye a beadwork design that looked something like the shapes the water and foam took. I know I do not always enjoy the everyday sewing of aprons and breechclouts and the tanning of hides. But I love to make fine regalia and do beading and quill-work decorations. And I saw that swirling pattern as clearly as if I were working it upon soft doeskin spread out on my lap!

Perhaps it was a kind of vision. Mother says the designs for her baskets often come to her in dreams. I am shy to ask her about this. Besides, she is so concerned these days with Snowbird, who is nine moons old now, but who does not seem to thrive.

Is it a vision Squant sent me of this eddying design? I wonder.

Because I do not have my birchbark with me, I am drawing the design I saw here in the sand at Montaup, so my hand can help my mind remember the way of it. Or is it the other way around?

Someday I will bead this pattern onto something important I am making.

LATER

The flies here at the oceanside come in great swarms, so Mother has smeared us all with ointment made from that red juice of the bloodroot plant she gathers every spring. Now we look very ruddy, but the flies are avoiding us.

THE NEXT DAY

This afternoon, while the other children here at the encampment were gathering rocks and driftwood and seaweed for the big cooking pit on the beach, Wootonekanuske and I slipped away into the forest that borders the shore so closely here. This peninsula is thick-wooded, right down to where the narrow line of beach and pebbles begins, and I could hear a squirrel scolding. "Chatter," we call him in our tongue, and this one had much to say for himself. I chased him just for the fun of hearing him scold. I knew there would be a clambake tonight, and no one would be wanting stew made from any stringy squirrel. Besides, I had not carried my bow with me.

To speak the truth, Wootonekanuske did not exactly slip away with me. She was just tagging along behind as usual on her short legs. My own legs are strong and getting scarily long, it seems to me, ever since I started my monthly cycle this past summer.

It was a sunny early autumn afternoon. As I ran after the squirrel the sight of the leaves just beginning to turn gold and scarlet and orange against gray rock ledges and the bright blue sky made my chest ache somehow, just because it was all so beautiful.

It is strange that even though I do not like my little sister following me around all the time, she cannot bear to be where I am not. Today I almost outran her in these strange woods, but I waited until she caught up. She whispered that we should not go too far from Massasoit's village. Wootonekanuske is always frightened those English

Coat-men will kidnap her if we get too far away from our people. She is only two years younger than me, and I keep telling her she ought to stand tall and be braver. I am sorry to say that I called her "Little Moss-for-Brains" and "Mouse-Heart"! But then I agreed to start back with her toward the encampment after all.

To tell the truth, I was a little afraid myself in those woods so far from home. And as we began to retrace our steps, I realized that in our running we had left a trail as plain as if we had dragged a slain deer behind us.

All at once, as we entered a clearing, we sensed at the same time there was something different about the forest. I pointed with my chin toward a nearby deadfall, and we stole over and crouched behind the loosely piled old branches. I remembered too late all my father's skulking lessons:

> Move with the motion of other things.
> Make noise only when there is some other
>   sound to cover it.

Now two Someones were coming. At least, I thought, they were probably not English, for they seemed to know all the same tricks we had been taught about moving quietly. Only if we listened closely could we hear them taking steps whenever the light breeze blew and rattled the leaves.

At last, two Indian boys appeared in the clearing. Though I had not seen them for more than a year and they had grown much taller, I knew at once they must be Wamsutta and Metacom, Massasoit's sons. We watched as they squatted down to examine our tracks, and soon Wamsutta shrugged and got up to follow our back trail. But Metacom, the younger one, just kept scanning the ground. Then he looked straight over at our brushpile and called in a low voice for his brother to come back. "They are right over here," he said, and Wamsutta returned, grinning, and started toward us.

At that I sprang up and demanded to know how those two dared to follow us like sneaking wolves. Did they not have the courage to come up on two Pocasset women face-to-face?

Wamsutta smiled. I am tall, but he is taller. He said he had seen no <u>women</u>, but that he and his brother had certainly heard two Pocasset <u>little girls</u> go crashing through the brush, making as much noise as a wounded moose.

Metacom stood up. He said softly that he was very sorry if they had scared us, but after all it was our own father who had sent them to find us.

I glared at him and said that nothing had scared us,

least of all two sneaky Pokanoket boys. Then I grabbed Wootonekanuske by the arm, and we walked as swiftly as possible back toward the shore and our people. This time, my sister and I took care to snap no twig, disturb no leaf. I did not deign to look behind us, but I was sure those boys were grinning. In Wamsutta's case, I am certain he was smirking.

I am sorry to say this, but I am not patient, and I do not like those boys. I am only sorry that I ran carelessly through the woods and gave them a way to trail us effortlessly.

LATER

I have a full belly and a full heart tonight. Tonight I think I might someday learn to be patient.

THE NEXT DAY

They say that when Squant and her husband, Maushop, and their children lived among us, the two were so gigantic that for food they would just scoop up whales off the coast and broil them whole on the beach. It is sad if

Squant and her family did not get to enjoy clambakes just because clams were too puny a food for those giant ones to eat. But who knows, maybe their whale-roasts were as much fun as our clambakes!

I know I ran off from the early part of those cooking-pit preparations yesterday afternoon. But what a joy it was to get away from those two Pokanoket boys and work with the other women and youngsters to cover the stones grown hot in the bonfire with armfuls of wet rockweed! I always love to hear the squishy float-bladders pop in the heat. On top of the seaweed we piled layers of clams and fish, with rockweed in between, and at last heaps of our sweet Mother Corn in her green-skirt husks. Finally we covered the whole pit over with yet more rockweed, and then we let the ocean-smelling steam cook all this good food. When we raked open the pit, everything was ready: golden corn, clams with their shells peeping open, and sweet-fleshed fish. Of course, Wamsutta and Metacom helped, too, but I whispered to my sister, "We must not even look at them!"

My dear friend Cedar and her family arrived in camp by the time we began our feast. She has a wide grin I could recognize from a hundred paces away! She and I sat side by side, though at first we hardly talked, we were so busy eating. We just smiled and nudged each other as we chomped corn and fish and slurped down clams from their shells. Dribbles of juice made our arms and hands shiny and clammy smelling. Afterward, all of us young ones raced over to the silvery freshwater stream that runs out of the woods and across the beach and empties into the sea. There we washed up, because if you try to rinse off in the salt water, it just makes everything stickier. The tide was starting to come in, and we squatted down at the shoreline on slippery rocks and waded a little in the bay, which is no longer warm enough to swim in. Then we all walked up toward the great council fires surrounded by wetus. We finished cleaning up the empty shells and corn-cobs and joined our families in the circle around the central fire. As the evening grew cooler with an autumn edge to it, we snuggled down in our bearskin robes.

There was dancing. Oh, the sound of the drum, and the voices joining in the dear old songs of thanks and joy, and the dancers circling the fire, their faces lit up one by one as they moved past us! The storyteller began just as full darkness fell. This time the one doing the telling was the old woman who is a great-great-auntie of Cedar. Her name is Willow, but everybody just calls her Nou'gou'mis, or Grandmother.

Last night the stories were about Squant and Maushop

and their children. We learned how Squant's eyes became square!

Tonight I am sleeping with Cedar and her family. She and I watched the dancing for a while and then crept over here into our bearskins and whispered and giggled until very late. Wootonekanuske tagged along, of course. When we told Cedar about those boys following us into the forest, she laughed, and then said thoughtfully she was not sure it was such a bad thing to be followed by boys like them. Well, they are her cousins, and she really likes them. All the while we talked, we could hear the crackle and roar of the great council fire, and our elders singing. But now even Cedar is fast asleep, and so I can have my thinking-time.

Here is how it was last night.

"Listen," the storyteller began, as she always must, *"here is something about Maushop and Squant."*

"Oh, good!" we all said loudly together, as we always do, to encourage her. I lay on my tummy between Wootonekanuske and Cedar, with my chin on my hands.

Next to my sister my mother sat cross-legged on a bear-skin, nursing Snowbird. In the silences between the parts of the story, we could hear Snowbird's lips smacking as she suckled our mother's rich milk. Since we have been here at Montaup, our baby sister seems stronger. My Auntie White Frost says that when our people come together to parlay and dance and listen to the stories and the singing, it brings us all better health.

"Now those two, Maushop and Squant, were very much larger than ordinary folk," the storyteller went on, *"and when our people first came upon them, on the easternmost shores of this land, beside the Sunrise Ocean, those two giant ones were very generous. Maushop shared with us the whales he fished up and broiled on the beach."* (And here, as I listened to Nou'gou'mis, I imagined what she was telling, and in the darkness I traced with my finger the shape of a whale in the sand.)

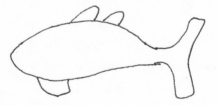

"Maushop told us when to plant crops, and he warned us when the big storms were coming.

"The people thanked Maushop with heaping baskets of tobacco, and to this day his pipe smoke makes the fog. When he knocked the ashes out of his giant pipe, a pipe with a stem far longer than the tallest pine, he made the island we call Nantucket, Far-Off-Among-Waves. Then he threw huge rocks into the ocean to give him stepping-stones from whence he might fish, and many a Coat-man's ship has run aground there, at that place the English call the Devil's Bridge.

"Countless are the tales of Maushop, but tonight I will speak of Squant, his wife, who watches over our girls and women, and why it is that she looks as she does.

"Once, Squant was so beautiful that all women were jealous of her, and all men except Maushop were angry because they could not have her for themselves. One late summer day she fell asleep in a sandy hollow in the dunes after picking beach plums. A bad-hearted man decided that if he could not have her, he would make her so that no one else would ever want her. He stole upon her with the shell of a razor clam in his hand, and quick as you can blink he slit her eyelids, snick-snick-snick, so that her beautiful green eyes became square-shaped when she opened them. She woke with a cry, wiping the blood from her lovely cheeks. By the time people came to help, it was too late to catch the man, who had fled down the beach and flung the clamshell back into the ocean.

"Ever since, Squant has worn her long black hair brushed forward over her face to hide her strange eyes. And yet the few *who have come across her on the dunes at twilight and seen her part her heavy hair and stare at them swear she is still awesomely beautiful, square eyes and all."*

THE NEXT DAY

Tonight, Cedar came to spend the night in our camp. Lying there in the dark we held hands and tried to remember exactly Nou'gou'mis's words about Squant, repeating the story over and over to each other, so someday we shall be able to tell it properly ourselves. Cedar forgot it was a razor clam the bad man used on Squant's poor eyelids. She said he used a flint knife, but Wootonekanuske and I both remembered better. I thought my little sister had been sound asleep during the storytelling, but it seems she was listening all the time. When Cedar said the part about the knife, Wootonekanuske bounced up right out of her bearskin and cried, "No, no, it was a clamshell, was it not, Weetamoo?" Yes, I told her, hush.

I can still see in my mind's eye Squant waking up on the beach with her poor cut eyes, and the bad man running down the beach and tossing that bloody clamshell off into the shallows.

I wonder, shall I ever meet Squant's square-eyed beauty face-to-face?

THE NEXT DAY

Tomorrow is our last full day at Montaup. There has been feasting and dancing and storytelling every night, and the elders talk all during the days. We know, Cedar and I, from listening at the councils where our elders pass the pipe and speak of troubles, that there is much talk among them of the Coat-men's cattle and pigs. The Coat-men set their animals free every day to roam outside their stout pens and stockades. Then these creatures happily trample our fields. The pigs root up our corn with their wet, snuffly snouts, and we children cannot scare them away so easily as we do the crows just by waving our arms and yelling. What is more, the Coat-men's cattle roam easily over the wide, grassy meadows we have carefully cleared for *attuks*, the deer, to browse in. Once the deer would come gratefully to graze in the meadows we prepared for them, and in turn they easily gave up their lives to us so that our people might have meat during the winter. Now the great clumsy mooing beasts muddy these open places and crop all the tender grass, and the deer hide far back in the woods. They have become much harder to hunt.

Massasoit shakes his head and says he has tried to tell the Coat-men to keep their beasts to home. But they say it is we who should take the trouble to build stout fences around all our fields, we who fence in no living thing, not plants or animals, either.

My father takes the pipe from Massasoit and smiles. I know what that smile means, for I have seen it many times. It means, "I told you so."

LATER THIS DAY

O Squant, grant me patience, but even more, grant me skill!

This afternoon, as we youngsters were gathering rockweed to spread over the beachside cooking pits for our final feast, those boys Wamsutta and Metacom edged near me and my sister. Wamsutta leaned close to me and whispered he had heard rumors that a certain little Pocasset girl could shoot an arrow straighter than any youngster. He said that he did not believe a word of it, but if I'd meet him tomorrow at dawn in that same clearing where he and Metacom discovered us cowering — Cowering! That was the word he used! — then we could test the truth of the matter.

He said this all with such a grin, it made me angry, and I threw a handful of sopping rockweed right into his face. Wootonekanuske and Amie gasped, but Cedar only laughed.

While Wamsutta spluttered and wiped the strands of seaweed from his eyes, I said he could count on seeing us Pocasset women there. Suddenly, his younger brother, Metacom, stepped forward and laid one hand on my arm and his other on Wamsutta's. He said we should settle the matter with marksmanship, not harsh words and flung seaweed. Then he added that each of us should think of what we might offer as a gift should the other person win the match.

I am almost certain I shall win, but if I do not, I believe I will present Wamsutta with a pot full of biting black-flies! I shall enjoy seeing the expression on his face.

THE NEXT DAY

Right now I am riding the swells, headed back home in our dugout canoe, clutching a wriggling puppy to my belly. I am happy to say I won the archery contest.

I want to remember the way it was. When we got to the clearing where we were to meet, the boys were already there and they had brought some of their friends as well as their little sister, Amie. She was carrying their baby brother Sunconewhew. As always, when I look at other little ones of Snowbird's age, I feel a tug at my heart when I see how much more robust they seem than she, but I had little time to dwell on that thought.

Wootonekanuske pulled at my arm as I began to stride straight out into the clearing. She shoved a rolled-up belt she had woven into the palm of my left hand and tucked my fingers about it. "Remember, you should have something to give him, whether you win or lose," she whispered, and I realized that was true. I just had not thought about it — I had been so busy practicing archery, even last night in my dreams.

"You keep it," I whispered back, "until this is over." She nodded and slipped away to stand with Cedar and Metacom and Amie and the others who had come to watch. Wootonekanuske and I were made to bring along Seal and Gull this morning, so my poor sister had her hands full with those twins. Finally she put them to building little wetus out of twigs, and they settled down.

Wamsutta was checking the strings on his full-sized bow of hickory, more than five feet long. I clutched my smaller bow, the one Father made especially for me. I knew his bigger bow meant Wamsutta would surely have a longer range, but I also knew I had a good eye and a steady hand.

Wamsutta's face was lit by the ruddy autumn dawn light. He looked up and pointed to a circle he had already drawn with dark pokeberry juice on the smooth trunk of a big birch about thirty paces away. He proposed we see who could come closest to the center of the circle the most often, using five arrows apiece. I agreed, and nocked my first arrow to my bow. I looked across the clearing at the target until somehow, as sometimes happens when you are shooting well, my arms and my eye and the arrow and the circle all seemed to come together. Then I let fly, knowing even before the arrow stood shuddering in the heart of the bark that my aim would be true.

Wamsutta's bowstring broke on his very first shot and unnerved him so much that he hit the target only two times, and I four.

Now we are coming into a stretch of very choppy water, so I will stop thinking for a while.

LATER

After our contest was over, when I could still feel the cold, nervous sweat running down my sides, Metacom stepped forward and touched me lightly upon my shoulder. "My brother has something for you," he said. Wamsutta nodded. "You shoot well," he said, grinning. He went over to a turkey-feather cloak he had thrown on the ground. The cloak was moving. He lifted it, and out tumbled a puppy. I guessed he would look like a muscular wolf when he was grown, but right now he was all wet nose and brown fur and rolls of fat. I knelt down beside him and rubbed his tummy. The puppy whined and licked the salty sweat off my palm.

"He is as plump as an *ohkuk*, round as one of Mother's clay pots!" I said.

"Why don't you call him Ohkuk, then," said Cedar, and Wootonekanuske nodded vigorously.

So now Ohkuk rides in my lap and squints his eyes in the salt spray and yelps when a wave washes over the side of the dugout. Father is pleased, for the more dogs a family has, he says, the better.

Father has never once asked me how I came by Ohkuk. Somehow, I have a feeling he already knows.

I will train Ohkuk to be a good watchdog, and teach him how to fetch a mallard when I shoot one from my canoe and it falls into the saltwater pond. How proud we shall be when we fetch it home for dinner. And, though I know such things sometimes have happened in times of great hunger, I whisper into his silky ear that no one will ever, ever eat him.

I was so absorbed in Ohkuk, I forgot to give the woven belt to Wamsutta as a gracious present from winner to loser. Later, in the bustle of our packing up and leaving, I thought I saw Metacom wearing it. How can that be? I wondered, but then we were off. In my joy at winning and what with Ohkuk squirming in my arms, I forgot to wonder more.

I am so glad to have my birchbark again!

Here is a picture of Ohkuk:

TAQUONTIKEESWUSH
HARVEST MOON
[EARLY OCTOBER]

Today we move inland to our winter village, Nemasket! It
is too cold and exposed to live here on the shore when the
autumn storms begin. So we roll up the reed mats that
cover the wooden frames of our wetus and go inland,
where it is more sheltered, and the deer hunting will be
better. I am going to be careful to roll my birch bark in with
the mats I will be carrying. I think no one will glimpse it,
and it is a secret. After we get to Nemasket, once again I
will take care to hide it well.

How I love the change of seasons, and our moving between these two sweet places! Here at Mettapoiset, our
plump little neck of land sticking into Narragansett Bay, it
is all fishing and swimming and the corn growing in wide
fields just out of reach of the salt spray, and we live out of
doors nearly all the time. I love it when, in summer, we
boys and girls alike sit on cornwatch platforms and clap
and sing and make loud noises to scare away the crows!

But I love it when this harvest moon comes, too. By
now at Nemasket the bittersweet vines will be burning
gold and orange in the swamps. Soon there will be deep
snow, and venison dripping fat over winter fires, and corn

stew to share around and people coming together. We youngsters will play snowsnake, and the grown-ups will gamble and tell the old stories and gossip about all that has happened since last winter.

Shall we see Cedar and Amie, Wamsutta and Metacom this winter at Nemasket? I wonder. But first we must move!

One week later
Nemasket

We have been busy setting up our winter village. We have different kinds of dwellings, mostly, for winter — larger longhouses, thirty or even fifty paces long, that will hold a few families, and with room for two or more firepits. We cover them with bark rather than reed mats, because bark keeps the cold out better. We are inside much together, when the winter turns fierce. My Auntie White Frost and her handsome husband, Tall Pine, and their little twins, Seal and Gull, will be joining us in our longhouse, along with Tall Pine's mother. An illness struck her many winters ago, and it twisted her face and stole her speech. Mostly now she sits and rocks on her bearskin. She is called Loon Woman, and that seems a good name for her because she makes noises like those blackheaded diving birds that rock on the waters. When something strikes her funny, she laughs her high, chuckling laugh, and when her old legs pain her, she moans. Wootonekanuske and I are both a little afraid of her, but Mother has told us that Loon Woman is very wise. She says Loon Woman's bright eyes and sharp ears follow everything that goes on in the longhouse.

Though I love the company and the closeness of my relations, it is hard to find any time to be by myself. But I have found a place here at Nemasket to do my thinking-times! It is a great gray rock covered with lichens, a rock nearly as big as a whole wetu. Sometime long ago one of the old ones chipped out a picture of a handprint on it, the size of a big man's hand. People call it Hand Rock, but few come here.

Who made that handprint, I wonder?

I sit on the rock, now warm in the autumn sun. I lay my own smaller hand over the worn carving and think of those who came before us, of someone who wished to say to me and others who pass by, "I was here!"

The pictures I make on my birchbark or draw in the sand are like that handprint, I think, though they are not visible for all to see, and they will not last so long. But they remind me that I was here, I saw this, I felt that, for good or bad, on this one day.

There is a sort of hollow underneath the rock, a kind of little cave, where I can safely stow my birchbark and cover it with a few leaves. Here is my picture of the picture on Hand Rock:

THE NEXT DAY

Tomorrow I plan to go with my father, Corbitant, about a half day's journey, as far as the fence that surrounds the place where those English Coat-men make their homes. He goes to talk with their leaders about selling our land.

Well, to speak the truth, I suppose I will not exactly be going <u>with</u> Father.

Rather, I will be skulking secretly along behind him and his party.

Even though everyone says I shall be sachem someday after my father, no woman or child among us is allowed to go among the English, and especially not to the place they now call Plimoth. I asked Father what kind of a name that was, and he said that Plimoth is just the name of some big Coat-man village that lies across the Sunrise Ocean. I like better our name, Patuxet, which speaks of the little water-falls near there. I love our good Wampanoag names that tell us something about a place!

— Patuxet, Little Falls
— Podunk, Place Where Your Foot Sinks into
  the Mire
— Winooske, Wild Onions
— Kennebunk, Long Sandbar

I have never been to Plimoth, but now that I am about to have fourteen winters and am almost grown, I am de-termined to go and see what those Coat-men live like. And as I am not invited on the parlaying party, I shall have to go by myself!

I know that Patuxet is partly forbidden because my fa-ther and other leaders do not fully trust the English to re-spect us women and children. There are other reasons, too, for it is a sad place. Long before I was born, there once stood here a large village of our own people, until the spot-ted sickness came among them. Our *powwaws,* our wise healers, say the first pale men who came over the Sunrise

Ocean to catch fish and to trade with us brought the sickness with them on their great sailing boats. Almost all our people who once lived on this beautiful hill overlooking the Sunrise Ocean died of that plague.

The Coat-men arrived on our shores a few years later. They came not just to fish and trade, but to settle. Before they decided on Patuxet, they tromped up and down our coastlines, looking for just the right place to build their Coat-man village. On one hillside they found carefully covered-over pits of seed-corn people were storing for the spring planting-time, and they scooped the kernels up and took all of it with them. That *weachamin*, that stolen corn, sustained the English through their first winter on our shores. How our people must have wept — both those who died in their fevers, and those who survived to hide back in the forests!

To mark today — or what I am planning for tomorrow! — I draw myself skulking behind my father and his warriors as he goes to parlay at Plimoth:

TWO DAYS LATER

Yesterday I met a woman of the Coat-people and watched a swan die without cause.

Now I am sitting on Hand Rock and trying to remember it all. I think this will take several days of remembering, for a great deal has happened. Besides, my mother is so cross about my being gone without permission for a whole day when chores wanted doing, she has assigned me extra tasks of hide-scraping and corn-shelling and mat-weaving. It is hard to get away to where I can be quiet and remember.

To begin with, I do not think I was very successful with my skulking. I say this because even though Father never looked back at the tangled undergrowth of blackberry and sumac and grapevines where I was crouching and sneaking along behind him and his party, every once in a while he would turn and shy a rock backward in my direction, and I could hear him laughing up ahead.

I think he knew I was there the whole time.

There is Mother calling! I know Wootonekanuske must have spied on me, and told her where I am.

But if that is so, how did Wootonekanuske get so clever as to sneak up on me?

LATER

I get away for a few minutes to creep back up to Hand Rock!

It is odd, for Father and Mother bade me to do all this, but somehow I know I must have these thinking-times without anyone else knowing, and I must not neglect my ordinary chores in order to slip away. I think Father and Mother want me to learn to seek out these times for myself, and it is as though finding that time were part of the task set for me.

But there, now I am sitting atop my safe rock, and I can be quiet and remember Plimoth.

It is a little Coat-man village surrounded by a high palisade of logs. All anyone can see from a distance is that fence and the top of one single look-out place they call the Common House, tall as an oak, and the smoke curling upward from their fires.

When we drew near, I hid in the ragged grove of trees well back from their fence and watched as Father walked through the great gates that swung open to admit him into the English town. Father says these Coat-men are eager to chop down trees for fires and to build their houses, and now after thirty-some winters of their living here there are no large trees of the ordinary wild kind close to their dwellings. We mostly use smaller trees for firewood, and every year we set fires and burn away undergrowth to make wide spaces between the big trees around our villages. It is pleasant to walk underneath that green canopy of our forests, and easy for hunters to espy attuks and *nahom*, the herds of deer and flocks of turkeys. But around Plimoth it is all bared fields or tangled scrubby woods.

Again! Here comes Wootonekanuske to fetch me.

LATER

At Plimoth, Father went to meet with those Coat-men chiefs named Myles Standish and William Bradford. The Standish one is the head of the Coat-men's army, and they say his shock of hair and beard were once as fierce orange as our *askutasquash*, our bright pumpkins. His hair has gone mostly white now, and he is a pumpkin frosted over, shrunken and ill-looking. Pumpkin-head is one of our people's names for him. He is said to have a fiery temper.

The Bradford one is taller and darker, though now he, too, has gone gray. My father says that at least he thinks before he talks.

Here is what the three of them looked like, walking through those big gates, as I spied on them from the woods:

My father went to parlay about land matters once more. These Coat-men make our people drunk and persuade them to trade away parcels of our land for this and that — for *wampum,* the beautiful shell pieces we use for money, for metal goods, or for cloth. Few of our people realize that the Coat-men all think that once you put your mark on a paper, the deed is done forever, and the land is lost to us.

I mean to understand more about this paper-signing business. I know Wamsutta and Metacom and their father, Massasoit, have thought about that, and maybe I shall ask Wamsutta the next time I see him.

Mother is still so cross with me for sneaking away and following Father to Plimoth! Sometimes I think the only one who really cares for me is Ohkuk. But he is a dog, and a puppy at that.

Today, I am still remembering Plimoth, and my strange time there.

After Father disappeared through the gates, there was nothing more to be seen from the woods where I was spying. So I crept toward the palisade, and I edged along it down the hill until I found a peephole in those closely driven palings that make up their fence. Suddenly, there I was, looking into the backyard of a Coat-man!

These Coat-men houses are so odd, I cannot imagine living in one. About them there are no circles, no gentle curves to wrap around you, the way our wetus curve, the way the beach curves, the way the grasses bend in the wind. The English build with severe corners and upright walls. It was strange to see that stiff, square house poking up from the softly rounded hillside.

There was the big box of the house, with smoke rising from another little box on the roof, and all manner of boxes otherwise. Over in one corner of the yard stood a medium-sized box, and I could hear coming from it the low cluckings and churrs of the birds that must be penned there.

Mostly, I could see that the yard was a place for growing things, but not the way we grow our corn and beans and pumpkins. In our gardens, the cornstalks hold up the twining beans, and the big green leaves of the pumpkins shade the roots of all three plants and keep them from getting too much hot sun. All the sister plants grow mingled together, and help one another.

Instead, the Coat-men who lived in this wetu had built still more boxes like square rock cages! The cages held soil, and here the plants grew in long lines laid out straight like bowstrings, one box for one kind of plant, another for a different sort.

Here is a picture of the Coat-man's garden:

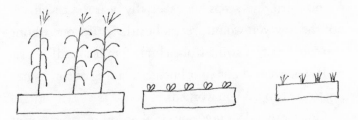

I must go back to our own longhouse now. Snowbird will be waking from her nap, and Mother will need help tending her. But oh, I have not yet told the most strange things about Plimoth!

O Squant, who protects us girls and women, please watch over Snowbird, my little sister.

Since we returned from Montaup and moved to our winter quarters, Snowbird keeps getting paler and more quiet. She is so different from the other children! I well remember when Seal and Gull were her age, how plump their arms and cheeks, and how they squirmed to be put down when we held them. I know Mother is worried, though she does not speak of it. But I can see it in the way she looks at Snowbird, and keeps her especially near to her. This is not the way you would treat a healthy child, one whom you could just let swing from a branch in her cradleboard while you went about your business, calling out and singing to the baby as you worked.

Our mother does not move in that sort of carefree way these days.

The next day

Well, the Coat-man's house proved to be a Coat-<u>woman</u>'s house, after all! I peeped eagerly through the gap in the fence at the English garden. I do not know the names and the uses of most of these Coat-men plants. But I am very curious about them. I recognized some things growing there. There were pale green plants with fleshy leaves, big and round as a man's head, like this:

Growing in a box right under my nose was something low and fragrant and very sweet-smelling, as well as a shrub whose gray-green leaves looked a little like spruce needles. I could tell just from the smells that these must be medicine-plants of some sort. I longed to know what teas and poultices could be made out of them, and what ills they might cure.

Just then a Coat-woman came out the door into her yard. She flung some grain she carried in her apron into the birds' box, crying, "Chickabiddy, chickabiddy, chuck

chuck chuck!" in a high voice. The speckled birds crowded about to peck at the food, and then that woman came walking straight toward me, where I crouched peeping at her from the other side of the fence. She was a small woman with frowning gray brows beneath her white cap. She carried a basket on her arm, and she took shiny little scissors from her apron pocket and began to gather the plants growing in the box right below my eyes. As she snipped them, their scent came up stronger to me. I heard her say, "Good day, lavender," and "Good day, rosemary," under her breath.

I know that Coat-man word *good day*. It is like our *quay*, hello, so I think *lavender* and *rosemary* must be the names of the plants, and she was greeting them. Despite her fearsome eyebrows, it made me feel good that this Coat-woman would talk to her garden just as we do.

Suddenly she looked up and stared straight at me through the chink. I had never meant for her to see me, but now it was too late. She was startled, but recovered herself quickly.

"Good day, Little Savage!" she said. "Do you care for some rosemary?" And with that she thrust a sprig of one of those plants through the chink straight at me. I gasped with fear, but I took it, and scrabbled backward from the fence. I could hear her laughing on the other side. I pressed the sprig of rosemary to my nose. What a pungent, clean smell it has!

I keep it now in the little deerskin pouch I always carry that has my special arrowhead made of white quartz, and some kernels of Mother Corn, and the gray river rock striped with red that my mother found the day she knew for certain she was carrying me.

I know that *savage* is one of their words for us, but I do not know exactly what it means.

I will tell the rest about Plimoth later.

THE NEXT DAY

Now comes the thing I saw at Plimoth I cannot forget, though I wish I could. There came noises overhead — a soft rush of wings and shrill cries drifting down from the sky. The Coat-woman within the fence and I without both looked up to watch four wild swans flying toward the inland marshes, where they forage and raise their young. My heart lifted to see those beautiful *wequosh*, those swans, at once so slim and so strong, beating their gleaming white wings and flying home.

Suddenly there came a noise, a loud <u>ker-whump!</u> from somewhere behind me. Black smoke and a stinking odor filled the air. I saw a ruined bird spiraling down, blood streaked across its breast, and then a young Coat-man, perhaps my own age, about a hundred paces from me, holding the kind of gun they call a fowling-piece up to the sky. I kept crouching in the tall grass, and I watched the young man run toward the fallen bird. He took one wing in each hand, spread his arms and flapped them, as though to make the poor thing fly again, and called out as if he were a swan, though his call would fool no bird, I think.

I have eaten swan. But this bird was so riddled with birdshot and torn up, there could be no eating from her, and the feathers so muddied and torn, they could never be used, either.

Why would anyone kill for the killing's sake?

Behind the palisade, I could hear the Coat-woman crying out.

I do not know what the English word means, but it seemed to my ears that she was crying, *"WICKED! WICKED! WICKED!"*

THE NEXT DAY

Well, there you have it. At the sound of the fowling-piece fired so close to the town fence, my father and several

Coat-men came rushing out. The boy's elders chastised him for his rashness at shooting so carelessly and so close to the settlement. But I do not think anyone said anything about the swan.

After that, I had a long, lonely skulk home from Plimoth. I have decided these Coat-men are a very mixed business, as Father has said all along. How can one know who will give you sweet-smelling gifts, and who will be outrageously violent?

PEPEWARR
WHITE FROST MOON
[EARLY NOVEMBER]

The view is so different at Hand Rock since most of the leaves have fallen from the trees. I can see the smoke of our village fires from here now.

Today I let Ohkuk follow me. Usually our dogs just stay around the wetus unless someone takes them hunting to run down deer or retrieve birds. Ohkuk is already getting to be more like a Wampanoag dog instead of an irresponsible puppy, and I do not have to worry so much about him barking and revealing my whereabouts. He is happy snuffling around in the leaves and chasing after the scents of squirrels and digging at woodchuck burrows while I do my thinking.

Yesterday Cedar and her family arrived here at Nemasket. Now we can start to plan some good times! They came a little later than usual this year because their Auntie Nou'gou'mis was too sick to travel. But now she is better, and we can hope for more good stories.

I have seen no sign of those two boys. Perhaps Massasoit and his family have decided to winter over elsewhere. I am sure my elders know, but I am a little shy to ask them. In a way, I am glad — what if Ohkuk wanted to go back to being Wamsutta's dog? Here is a picture of Ohkuk following me:

THE NEXT WEEK

Cedar and I have a plan. We are not invited on the usual hunting parties, so we are going to go deer-hunting by ourselves! I know we will get in trouble for doing this, as hunting is not considered women's work, but perhaps that will not matter so much if between the two of us we are able to bring home a fat attuk. I am so impatient with only being allowed to do the dressing of the meat and the tanning of the hides!

Father says the Coat-men's presence has driven the deer farther and farther away. He is soon going to lead a party of men and boys to some good deer-hunting spots our people have prepared off to the west of here. There the trees grow widely spaced in the old way, and no Coat-man village is near.

But Cedar and I have seen the tracks of a small herd, a buck and three does, not far down the river from our village. We will sneak out before dawn tomorrow and meet at the river with our bows and arrows, to see if those deer come down to drink.

There is one problem. We have not been taught the proper prayers to make ourselves ready for the hunt. With squirrels and rabbits and ducks, Father has taught me how to ask for permission to hunt them and how to give thanks if I am successful, but there is more to be done somehow about hunting deer. Cedar worries about this, but I told her we could just pray very humbly to Manitou, the Great Spirit who created the game animals and all else, to make it right. She is doubtful, and so am I at heart, but I feel we must try this. If we are to be sachems, should we, too, not be capable of feeding our people?

The next day

O Squant, what a disaster! Why did you not somehow send a sign to stop me?

I suppose you would say you did warn me, and that you were the source of that doubt in my heart I spoke of yesterday.

I have forgotten to ask you for patience for many days now. And there, I know, lies much of the trouble.

Well, here is how it went. It all started off as a great adventure, with Cedar and I stealing away from our village before daybreak and following the river. There was heavy frost underfoot, but our moccasins stuffed with moss were thick enough to keep our feet warm. It was very beautiful to see the morning mists rising from the river, and then the bare lines of the trees reflected in the water by pink dawn-light.

Sure enough, the buck was leading his family down to the water's edge, and with our bows and arrows in hand, we edged up as close as we could. We knew we would have to be very close indeed to bring down even a small doe with bow and arrow.

Just then we heard a beaver slap his tail in warning across the river, and all four deer broke for cover. In panic, Cedar and I both let fly our arrows, not very carefully, and one of them — mine or hers, neither of us is sure — pierced the smallest doe's neck. She stumbled, but got her footing again and kept on running with the others. Though we tried to trail them, we soon fell far behind in the tangle of woodsy swamp that borders the river. Back-tracking, we could see the splashes of her blood on the fallen leaves.

So now instead of meat for our families and praise for us, there is a wounded animal running about in pain. We both wept on the way back to Nemasket, and Cedar ran to her family longhouse as soon as we reached the village.

LATER

I did what I knew I must: I confessed to Father what Cedar and I had done. He said nothing — another of his terrible silences. He just nodded and picked up his bow and motioned me to follow him toward the river.

I showed him where our shooting had taken place, and he waved me back toward the village, while he set off on the deer's trail. I spent a miserable day, without complaining, doing all and more than Mother asked.

In the midafternoon, when the shadows were lengthening, Father walked up to our longhouse with the dead doe on his shoulders. He told me he had tracked her to where she lay wounded in a thicket and then he mercifully stole her breath — that is, he smothered her quickly. He says we will talk tomorrow, he and I.

In the meantime, I have to help Mother skin and clean and butcher the doe.

It will be one of the saddest tasks I have ever done.

THE NEXT DAY

Father led me back to that same place along the river where we shot the doe. We sat on a fallen log by the water's edge in silence. Again the beaver slapped his tail to tell his kin there were human beings about, and it brought back yesterday morning to me strongly.

Finally, Father spoke. He told me it had taken him a long time to decide what to say to me. He said that he thought I had learned some lessons already; about consulting with one's elders, and about the need to learn how to kill a creature quickly and with compassion, rather than clumsily.

But he said most important of all were the bonds among Manitou and other spirit-beings and the animals and our people. There are old stories that tell us how to behave, and there are prayers I have not learned, and many other things we do that show our thanks and respect.

As he spoke, I realized I did know about some of those acts already, such as the way we always burn a bit of the deer's fat on the fire before we eat, so the rising smoke can be a thank-you offering to Manitou, Creator of All. And I have seen how our people carefully gather and bury the innards of every slain deer that feeds and clothes us, and supplies us with bone for tools, so as to return its spirit to the earth. I remembered with shame that Cedar and I had been so excited yesterday, we really had not even tried to garble together any kind of prayer at all.

If we do those things, Father went on, the animal spirits will keep coming back to us, reborn into their new deer bodies, and our children and our children's children will be fed. He paused.

"But if a Wampanoag omits these things," he said, "it is just as bad as when a foolish child of the Coat-men kills, oh, say, a swan for no reason." And he looked down at me. I gasped then, and I knew that he knew I had been there at Plimoth that day.

Then he smiled and said there were certain lessons he thought he must begin to teach me, because it might indeed be true that one day I would have to be a hunter. More than a hunter, a trusted councillor. But a great part of that teaching was about the patience I seem to not be doing so well with lately. "You will never lack for heart and fire, Daughter," he told me, "but as for judgment . . ." He shook his head and sighed, saying, "It will come."

THE NEXT DAY

I spent most of the day beginning the job of tanning the doeskin. I lugged the hide down to the river and submerged it there, weighed down by stones, until the hair was loosened enough for me to scrape off. I thought of how the doe had drunk from this same river in her last moments. And I wondered the whole time I was working whether what Cedar and I had done would keep this doe and the other deer from coming back and yielding their lives up to us in the future.

THREE DAYS LATER

I am still tanning the doe's hide. I made a paste of the doe's own liver and brains and some of the urine I pressed from her bladder. I spread this all over the hairless skin, and now I am working a stone back and forth, back and forth, over the smelly hide to make it soft and pliable. Ordinarily I would complain, but I am not complaining today. I must make sure this doe's life is not wasted.

A WEEK LATER

First snowfall! This one only came up as far as my ankles, but it looked so beautiful dusting the longhouses and the pine boughs, and it was plenty deep enough to play in. Wootonekanuske and I were out early, romping with Ohkuk. Our village dogs love to follow the delicate little tracks of the field mice and then pounce on the place where the prints disappear because the creature has burrowed under the snow. Ohkuk has yet to catch a mouse, and after a while he gave up and began chasing the snowballs Wootonekanuske and I and the other children were lobbing at one another. Seal and Gull giggled and rolled in the snow. I packed snowballs for them to throw, and they were delighted to toss them a few paces. I think the little ones will be good at this when they are older.

As for Wootonekanuske, she does not have a very good aim, and she cannot make her snowballs go very far. I am trying to teach her how to use her whole arm when she throws, not just the part from her wrist to her elbow.

But I truly did not mean to hit my sister in the face with a snowball. I was aiming at her back, but she turned around suddenly at just the wrong moment. She spluttered and cried, and asked if I always had to be throwing things in people's faces. I apologized and helped her wipe off the snow. I must say for once she did not run to tell Mother.

This morning was the first time I have seen Cedar since our misadventure. I think her family has been keeping her close by their longhouse, as I have been kept. I am sure at least one of her elders gave her a lecture such as Father gave me. In any case, we had no chance to speak among ourselves, and she stayed to play for only a short time. I hope she will forgive me for getting her into such a scrape. I think we both have learned a hard lesson.

THE NEXT DAY

When we walk to the river in these mornings to fetch water, we do not yet have to break through hard ice. But Father says this is going to be a cold winter, judging from the signs like the thickness of the dogs' fur, and how wide the black stripes were on the wooly-bear caterpillars last summer. The fatter the black band, the harder the coming winter. Here is how the caterpillars looked:

Soon it may be difficult for me to get up to Hand Rock. Of course I can go anywhere on snowshoes, but not as quickly as on foot in good weather, so there would be more time spent in snowshoeing than thinking. I will have to figure out another place to be private and stow my birchbark, a place closer to home.

But the deep of winter coming on brings me graver worries. If indeed it is a fierce one, how will the feebler among us survive it? I think of dear Nou'gou'mis the storyteller, who has lived more than eighty winters, but who was very ill this past autumn.

Most of all I think of Snowbird, still so thin-limbed as she comes near her first twelve moons. Because she was born in Paponakeeswush, the Winter Month, she was named for the cheerful little plump birds who survive even the toughest weather, who twitter around our village in big flocks in winter. But Snowbird is not plump, and she does not seem to have the energy to be cheerful. Her beautiful big eyes follow me whenever I am working around the longhouse and she is hanging in her cradle-board.

Two days later

At last I have seen Cedar long enough so that we might talk. We met by the river, where we had both gone to draw water, for the snow is not deep enough yet for us to just scoop it up and melt it. "Quay," she said softly, and "Quay," I replied. After we shyly said our hellos, she flashed her wide grin and we hugged each other.

I am so glad Cedar bears me no grudge!

As we were walking back along the frosty path to the village carrying our pots of water, I asked if her parents were angry with her. Yes, she said, but not so angry as they would have been if she had not told them the truth about the doe. Her father and my father talked, she tells me, and her father told her that they are planning somehow to give the two of us the extra knowledge we may need to be hunters, just as my father hinted.

This excites us greatly.

Of course Cedar and I have already had our women's initiations, back when we started our monthly cycles. Then we were taught many things. We were each taught how our bodies work, and how to care for ourselves in those times. For those few days, the Manitou, the spirit, is strong within us. But we were also taught about how the wetu is the family's center place, and the woman the center of it. We were told about why it is our special woman's duty to till the ground and tend to our gardens, because our own bodies are like the earth, and bring forth the new crop of our people.

It was very beautiful, even though I am not certain I understood all of it. I think there are things a person must just grow into understanding.

Two days later

Cedar and I have been wondering if our fathers mean for us to go through the boys' initiation, exactly. It is not very common for girls to be summoned to go through this. We have heard it whispered that to become a respected councillor, a boy must go through a great ordeal. The Powwaw takes the chosen boys into a special wetu. Each boy has to expel all evil from his body by drinking a bitter tea, and vomiting, and then swallowing more bitter tea, until he is cleansed. Then he must go alone and nearly naked into the forest with very little food and water. There he must seek to make contact with the spirits. Sometimes they come to him in dreams, and sometimes they appear directly before him, as animals or birds or people, and tell him things. Sometimes the spirits may take him on strange journeys that seem to last for years, but when he awakens, it will still be only dawn of the next morning in this world, and he finds himself lying cramped and stiff on the same ground where he lay down the night before. They say that the lives of those who encounter a spirit are changed forever.

If that is what our elders say we must do, we can do it, I told Cedar.

She said she was not so sure, and I knew she was remembering me telling her how easily we would be able to kill a deer.

In my heart, I, too, am not sure we can do what is required. But I know we must try.

I cheer myself up by thinking that if this ordeal is something that boys like Wamsutta and Metacom can survive, surely Cedar and I have a chance!

The doeskin is tanned now, pliant and supple as you could wish. I hold it close in my lap and think about patience.

QUINNE KEESWUSH
THE LONG MOON
[EARLY DECEMBER]

More snow. When it is falling down in big fat flakes, Ohkuk looks up in wonder and barks if one lands on his black nose. By now the snow comes halfway up my calf, and we need not go to the river for water. Instead, I get to see Cedar every morning when Wootonekanuske and I are outside bringing in firewood and scooping up snow for meltwater in our clay pots and baskets.

No one has said more to either of us about teaching us the way of hunters and councillors, and that is something one simply cannot ask Father or Mother or the Powwaw about. They would not answer you at all, or else they would only say that the most important things take place in the fullness of time. But I am longing to know when it might happen, and what we will have to do!

Oh, my. I realize what impatient thoughts I have just been thinking.

Please, Squant, give me patience.

Yet another big happening is coming. Everyone is talking about how there is to be a great gathering here at Nemasket during *Lowatanassick*, the midwinter season when the nights are longest, and Mother says we must already begin to prepare for the feasting. That means much dried corn-grinding for me and Wootonekanuske, at the very least. I know I will need patience to do that much work! But right now, I am thinking more about how the work leads to the feast, and how corn-grinding is work my sister and I both do well, and how good it will be to do it in company with her and our mother and our Auntie White Frost, with Loon Woman snug in her corner making approving noises to urge us on, and the snow spitting against the bark roof of our longhouse.

THE NEXT DAY

I have been dreaming about the Midwinter games, especially snowsnake, the one I love best. We dig a long trough in the snow and pour water over it to make it extra icy. Then we take turns skittering our slim wooden sticks painted like snakes as hard as we can down the length of the trough. Whosoever's stick slides the farthest wins.

I must say I am pretty good at this game. I may not be as tall as many of the bigger boy players, but I have a good sense of just how to aim my snake down the slick runway, and I put both my shoulders into it when I thrust my snake away from me and whisper to it, "Go, go, go!"

I imagine that Massasoit and his family will come here then. I wonder if there will be a chance to play snowsnake with those two boys this midwinter? Here at Nemasket, many of the Pocasset children will not play with me. It is because they are afraid of being beaten by me. But I am guessing that Wamsutta might be willing to play snowsnake against me, even though I bested him at archery just last fall.

As I go about my ordinary chores of weaving mats and grinding the corn we just fetched inside from our storage pit, I imagine sitting in the great longhouse we will soon be making, one that will hold as many as a hundred of us, with several firepits down the middle, and smoke rising up through the smokeholes. I am thinking about corn stew, and how good the broiling venison and geese will smell as their sweet fat drips in the fire. I dream about playing snowsnake, and the sound of the drum, and people singing the winter gathering songs. I dream of listening to Nou'gou'mis telling stories, perhaps some more stories of Squant.

Most of all, I dream about what it will be like to learn to be a hunter and a councillor.

Here is a picture of me playing snowsnake:

THE NEXT MORNING

A hard night.

Oh, Squant, please grant Snowbird your protection.

Snowbird almost never cries, but last night she whimpered softly from the middle of the night until dawn. Wootonekanuske and I kept checking to see whether her diaper padding of soft milkweed fibers needed changing, and Mother repeatedly offered her the breast and wiped her face, but nothing seemed to help. Her breathing came hard, and when we took her out of her cradleboard we could watch her thin chest rise and fall. Finally we told Mother she must get some sleep. My sister and I took turns sitting up by the embers of the fire and rocking Snowbird in her cradleboard in our arms, quietly singing lullabyes.

> *Little bird, little bird,*
> *tuck your head beneath your wing.*
> *Little bird, little bird,*
> *time to sleep.*

I sang, and at long last Snowbird slept. I hung her cradleboard up on its peg and crept under the bearskin robe beside Wootonekanuske. This early morning my sister and I fell asleep with our arms around each other, and there was no poking or teasing whispers.

I do not know how exactly to say this, but sometimes it seems to me as though Snowbird lives halfway with Squant, or at least halfway not in our world. New babies often seem to have a distant look, as though they were remembering all sorts of things we older ones have forgotten. Soon, though, they begin to take a keen interest in this side of the world, and then that look leaves them. But our Snowbird has never lost it.

Here is Snowbird asleep in her cradleboard:

Mother spoke to the Powwaw today to ask if he might do something about Snowbird. We all had to leave the long-house for a while so he could spend time alone with Mother and the baby. We settled Loon Woman comfortably in Cedar's family lodge. She made worried noises, for she lay, awake all last night along with us, listening to Snowbird's fretful breathing. Wootonekanuske and Auntie White Frost and the twins and Father and I lingered about outside, and from within we could hear the Powwaw asking questions and praying. Later Mother told us how first he made a tobacco offering to Manitou the Creator, the Great Spirit, and then he blew the smoke about our sister and prayed. Next he took her gently out of her cradleboard and unwrapped her. He felt her body carefully all over. He listened to her breath and felt her pulse, and for a long time he put first one ear and then the other to her chest. At last he looked up at Mother. He rewrapped our baby in her rabbitskin blanket, and then he told Mother to call our family back inside.

The Powwaw always scares me. I know him for the man he is during his ordinary life — Red Hawk is his name, and he is the kindly father of two of my friends. But when he is dressed up as the Medicine Man, with his red and black face paint and his clamshell earrings, he looks fearsome indeed, and it is plain that the spirits have entered into him.

He told us it is Snowbird's *wuttah,* her heart, that is the problem. He believes there is a leak there somehow, so that the rivers of her blood and breath cannot flow strongly through her body. My father asked him if there is medicine for such a problem. The Powwaw only shook his head. No, he said, not for this thing. He says there is only medicine to help Snowbird travel back into the spirit world when the time comes, and medicine to help us, her family, accept her passing. But he says her heart cannot be mended.

My mother wept, and Father asked the Powwaw how long he thought we might have Snowbird with us. He said gently that no person could tell the time, but he thought probably not much longer than the days when the new leaves will appear.

I feel unready for this great change, and I am ashamed.

When I think that a day or so ago I was all wrapped up in thoughts of beating the boys at snowsnake!

Please give me patience, Squant, and watch over Mother and Snowbird.

Two days later

Yet more snow, so that now it comes up to my knee, and there is no easy way to get up to Hand Rock. I am glad I brought my birchbark down here to the village yesterday. I could think of no good place to hide it except under the sleeping mats Wootonekanuske and I share, so there it rested for a day. Now I have sneaked it outside to this alder thicket by the frozen river, and here is where I will do my thinking-time when the weather is fair enough to be outside.

Snowbird seems no worse. If anything, she is a little better. She has been eating a little more, and sleeping more soundly at night. So perhaps Squant is helping her, or maybe the Powwaw was mistaken after all.

Today, none of my friends could come walking or play outside in the snow. It seems lately as if everybody, even my dear Cedar, is kept busy fashioning wampum beads and stringing them. This wampum-making business has grown worse and worse, my father says.

Wampum is the beads made out of our ordinary whelk and quahog shells, both the white and the purple parts. We make pretty strings or belts of it. Sometimes we bead whole designs that mean things, so that a belt with a picture of a turtle next to an eagle could mean the friendship of two bands for whom those creatures were special. Then, too, we have always used it for exchange, or for trading for goods.

If I want to trade for something valuable, a fine puppy like Ohkuk for example, and I cannot give the owner something like corn or beaver pelts in exchange, I can give instead a certain number of strings of wampum — the purple is more valuable than the white — and the owner will accept that in trade. Mostly, though, we use it for special ceremonies — when a young man's family pays a dowry to his bride's family so the couple can marry, or when we mark an important exchange, like granting a treaty to another band allowing them to fish in our waters.

Anyway, here is what is different now. When the Coat-men came over the Sunrise Ocean, they left behind most of their own kind of money. Theirs is shiny and hard, with pictures and writings on bright circles of metal. In a short while they fell into the custom of using our wampum instead of their own English coins. These Coat-men use wampum for every little dealing, and there is never enough to supply them. So now many of our people spend their spare time at wampum-making, instead of at our usual arts of weaving and beading and pottery-making and basketry.

Father says it will end badly, for more and more of the Coat-men come pouring into our land every year, and now he hears that they have built places to melt down metal. Soon they will have their own sort of shiny coins again, and those of our people who have put all their energy into wampum-making will no longer be able to use it for trading with the Coat-men.

Here is a picture of wampum, and of some Coat-men coins:

TWO DAYS LATER

I have got hold of some especially fine wampum beads, both white and deep purple, from Cedar. I am going to sew them on a sash I will cut from the doeskin, and the design I will make is the one I saw in my mind's eye that day on our voyage over to Montaup. I do not yet know what I will do with it — perhaps give it to Father to wear at council meetings. But somehow I feel good doing this with a part of the doeskin.

THE NEXT WEEK
LOWATANASSICK
MIDWINTER
[EARLY JANUARY 1654]

Now in the dead heart of winter our people have come to-gether, and it is joyous!

This is the time when we make our winter accounting, and go over together all that has happened since last year. People will be remembering the big meteor shower of last summer, or telling about how the spring salmon fishing was especially good last year over to the northwest at Peskeompskut, that waterfall so thunderous, we call it Exploding Rocks. There are some of our elders who can recite by memory all the things that have been especially noticed for every year, beginning back in the time when Manitou first created us, and going all the way up to now! The Coat-men's writing is supposed to help them remember things, but my father says writing or no writing, they quickly forget their promises, and much of what has happened to them as well.

All last week we were busy building the special longhouse here at Nemasket. It is a hundred paces long, as long as a whale! It can hold nearly all of us who are gathered here when there is a council, or when there is storytelling, or when the menfolk are playing at our gambling game we call Hubbub, and people crowd around to watch and cheer on the players. Even as far away as the river I can hear them shouting, "Hub, hub, hub, hub!" — "Come! Come! Come! Come!" — as they toss the five half-painted bones in the basket tray and bet on how many pieces will land with their black sides up. My father has the reputation of being especially lucky at this game, and yesterday he came back to our longhouse with five strands of wampum he won. He may scorn the craze for wampum-making, but he does not scorn winning wampum from playing Hubbub!

Here is a picture of the five Hubbub bones in their tossing basket:

THE NEXT DAY

Massasoit, the great Yellow Feather, and his family are here! They have come to our midwinter gathering! There are even people who have come from as far north as Saugus. That boy Winnepurket, son of the sachem there, is among them. He smiles shyly and hangs back when we are in a group. Sometimes I think he, like Snowbird, is not very well.

Perhaps I should more properly call this Massasoit's winter gathering, since he is the honored Sachem over all the bands of us Wampanoag people. In any case, I spied those boys Wamsutta and Metacom this morning when I went out to get snowmelt water. I noticed that Metacom was still sporting the belt Wootonekanuske wove. Ohkuk came with me, as he does every morning, and he licked Wamsutta's hand when he kneeled down to pat him. "Well, little Pocasset girl, it looks like you know enough to keep a puppy alive," he said, rubbing Ohkuk's furry head. It is true, Ohkuk has grown almost twice as big since we have been here inland at Nemasket.

While Wamsutta patted Ohkuk, I asked him if he would like to play at snowsnake later, after he and his family were settled in. A slow grin spread over his face. "Do you mean play snowsnake against some little Pocasset girls?" he asked.

"No, I mean against Pocasset <u>women</u>, with strong bow arms and better aims than most," I said. I flounced back to our longhouse with my jar of water, and Ohkuk bounced along through the snow at my heels. Wamsutta called after me, saying that snowsnake was quite a different game from archery, one where bowstrings that accidentally snapped would not figure in.

I do not know if this game will ever come about, and I barely care.

LATER THIS DAY

I have been thinking of my father's saying that this business of wampum-making might change the very way our people live. They pile up great shell-heaps in order to make their amounts of wampum and then exchange them for Coat-man goods they prize, such as woven cloth and iron kettles.

Father often says we should all go on wearing deerskin clothes and cooking in our baskets and clay pots, no matter what.

In my spare time I am working on my wampum sash. It almost seems to bead itself, the design is so deeply set in my mind.

LATER THAT NIGHT

I am resting in my bearskin ready for sleep and I am thinking, and I must confess a secret truth.

Sometimes I myself wish for certain things the Coat-men have. I can see that their iron kettles are easier to cook in. Cedar's family has one, and it never bursts apart as our clay pots sometimes do when we suspend them over the fire to boil our stew.

The cloth the Coat-men weave and sew from different strange plants is very soft and supple to the touch. They dye it bright colors that catch my eye, and their shiny needles are stronger than the ones we whittle out of deer bone.

And oh, then there are the beads! I have only seen them once or twice, for the Coat-men at Patuxet dress very plainly. But some people among them in other villages have beads made of something called glass. These beads are shinier than wampum. Cedar has a handful of them that some Coat-man gave her father in exchange for seed corn. They are brilliantly colored, red and green and blue and yellow and mottled — and how they seem to catch fire in the sunlight!

When Cedar spills them out of her pouch to show us girls, I long to touch those beads.

And I confess I should like to sew them with an iron needle onto soft bright cloth, and make a picture — of yellow sunflowers, perhaps, or a cardinal bird, or the red stems and white flowers of bloodroot.

Purple and white wampum beads are the best for what I am doing now, sewing onto the doeskin that strange pattern I saw in my mind when I looked at the waves on our way over to Montaup. But I cannot help thinking about what other things I might do with those shining glass beads.

And I wonder, too, about the writing, the marks that the Coat-men use that are not pictures, and yet seem to say so much.

Maybe there could be a way to do that, to work with those Coat-man things and still not give up being a Wampanoag.

THE NEXT DAY

I spent most of the morning with my sister and Mother preparing food for our great feast tomorrow. Wootonekanuske and I began to quarrel over who would do which task. But then Snowbird started to cry, and Mother looked at us across the longhouse so wearily, we stopped our bickering then and there. We agreed to take turns grinding the dried corn, that endless task, and chopping up the cranberries and sweetening them with delicious dollops of maple syrup. I think you can guess which job we both preferred! I suggested that first I would grind the corn and she could mince the cranberries, and then we would switch around. Wootonekanuske agreed. I did not point out to her that by the time it was my turn to take over the cranberries, it would also be time to begin mixing in the syrup!

We do not cook the cranberries for this dish. We just crush the ripe berries, stir in the syrup, and set the pot out to chill in a snowbank for a while. I love to eat almost anything, but this relish is my favorite of all the foods we eat in wintertime. It is sweet and bitter all at once, and the cranberries are even brighter red than those red English glass beads I admire!

THE NEXT AFTERNOON

I am ashamed.

I lost today at snowsnake both to Wamsutta, who won, and to Metacom, who finished right behind him. I came in third, and Cedar fourth, and a whole string of boys behind us, including Winnepurket. Wootonekanuske played, too, but she finished far behind. She complained that her snake-stick was crooked, but I do not think that is where the trouble lay. I think she needs to complain less and practice more.

For a winner's present, I gave Wamsutta corn-cakes I made with some of last summer's dried strawberries kneaded in. At least he did not make fun of the simplicity of my gift. But of course, he could not resist teasing me. "Well, little archer," he said, and grinned, "when the conditions are equal, we see who wins!"

But the conditions are not equal! Wamsutta is simply older and bigger!

I wish for my arms to grow longer, and my back stronger. I am trying to be patient, but I hate to lose at anything, and with a little more practice and a bit more height, I know I could beat both of those boys.

Wamsutta offered me a rabbit skin for a loser's gift. I did not want to keep his gift, and I immediately handed it over to Wootonekanuske. She smoothed the soft gray fur and said we could sew it into a new warm coverlet for Snowbird. So be it.

THAT NIGHT

Tonight before the storytelling began, our fathers announced in the council meeting that Cedar and I are to go through a special learning ceremony after the full moon of Paponakeeswush, Winter Month. I was almost too excited to eat, but I forced myself, for I know that whatever happens, I will need to be very strong for what is coming in my life. I stared down into my carved wooden bowl at the stew my mother and I had made from dried venison and onions and parched corn. I knew this stew probably held meat from the very doe Cedar and I had slain so clumsily, and once again I silently asked her for forgiveness. Then I ate. With the help of the doe's flesh and her spirit, I can survive this lesson, and through it learn to do better. Perhaps the honor I am doing her skin with my wampum work will help, too.

It is late. Munna'mock, Grandmother Moon, set long ago. I will remember about the storytelling tomorrow.

THE NEXT DAY

Our storyteller last night was not Nou'gou'mis, but a guest from the north of here. His name is Gray Wolf, and he is one of the Abnaki, the Dawn People, who visit us now and then to trade our seed corn for their animal skins. Massasoit himself invited Gray Wolf to tell a story. The Wampanoag and the Abnaki languages are similar, and there are many words we share. Gray Wolf is so accustomed to coming south to trade with us, he has gotten to know our speech very well.

Winter nights are always the best times for storytelling. Our bellies are full of venison stew and corncakes and cranberries. The big longhouse smells of burning pine logs and the tobacco with which the elders have blessed our gathering time. We all snuggle down in our robes to listen. *"This is a story about Glouskabi,"*

Gray Wolf began, and we all said, *"Oh, good,"* to encourage him.

I think Glouskabi is the name the storyteller's Abnaki people call Squant's husband, Maushop. At any rate, Glouskabi is a large, powerful being, very much like him.

Here is the story Gray Wolf told us:

"A long time ago, when the world was new, Glouskabi lived with his Grandmother Woodchuck in a comfortable wetu in the forest. Every day he would go out to hunt and bring home game so his granny could make a delicious stew for the two of them.

"One day Glouskabi went out hunting and he had no luck at all. The same was true the next day and the next. Each time he set forth, the squirrel and the rabbit, the deer and the bear, and the moose could hear him coming, and they would hide themselves so well and so quietly, he could not find them.

"After some days of this, Glouskabi grew tired of his bad luck at hunting, and he went home to his Grandmother Woodchuck.

"'What is wrong, my Grandson?' she asked, sitting upright and showing her big front teeth in a worried way.

"Glouskabi replied, 'Grandmother, I am having no

luck at all at hunting. Would you please make me a game bag out of the hair of your own belly? Perhaps that will bring me luck.'

"'All right, Grandson,' Grandmother Woodchuck said. She plucked out all her belly hair and from it she wove a game bag and gave it to Glouskabi. 'Use it well,' she cautioned him. He thanked her and went back to the forest.

"When he got far inside the woods, he looked around. There were still no animals in sight, not so much as a deer's hoofprint or rabbit's scatter of round droppings. Glouskabi decided to play a trick.

"'Animals!' he bellowed. 'All you animals! Listen to me! The world is just about to end, and you will all drown or be blistered by fire unless you jump into my magic game bag right now!'

"The animals heard him, and they were frightened. One by one, from the littlest field mouse to the hulking moose, they all clambered into the game bag, and the wonder of it was that Grandmother Woodchuck's magic bag stretched wide enough to hold all the animals of the forest. Then Glouskabi tied up the bag and brought the huge bumping and squeaking and bellowing bundle home to his granny.

"'There,' he boasted, as he laid it on the floor of their lodge. 'I have got all the animals in the forest in here, and

I will never have to go hunting again! Now we can just reach in the bag and pluck out a fat rabbit or a deer whenever we want, and we shall eat very well!'

"But Grandmother Woodchuck shook her head. 'No, no, Grandson,' she said. 'Animals cannot live inside a game bag, not even a magical game bag. They need to be out in the world drinking from the streams and foraging and mating and raising their baby animals so there will be animals to feed and clothe those who come after us.

"'Besides,' she added, 'the more you hunt those animals, Grandson, the more resourceful you will get, and the more they are hunted by you, the more resourceful they will get. That is the Creator's way of keeping all of us strong and sharp-minded. So let those animal people free from your game bag, and you go back to hunting in the ordinary way. That is how the Creator intended things.'

"Glouskabi did as Grandmother Woodchuck told him, and that is why we are able to eat venison stew and sleep under bearskins this very night, because those animals have continued, and so we have continued."

THAT NIGHT

I have been thinking a lot about the game bag story. It is almost as if that Abnaki visitor told it especially for Cedar and me, just before we are brought into being hunters and councillors. I like especially that end part, where Grandmother Woodchuck says that hunting and being hunted keeps both us and the animals strong and clever.

Here is a picture of Glouskabi and his game bag:

PAPONAKEESWUSH
WINTER MONTH
[LATE JANUARY 1654]

No more snow has fallen, though it is bitterly cold. Snowbird still does not thrive, but she is no worse. It feels empty here, now that so many people have gone back to their own villages after our midwinter gathering. Wamsutta and Metacom are still here for a few more days.

I do not like to say it, but in a strange way I will miss those boys. Of course we have no shortage of boys here at

Nemasket, but there is something about debating and teasing with Wamsutta and Metacom that makes me feel sharper and more alive. It is a little like the story about Glouskabi and the game animals. When things are too easy, it is not as much fun, and I grow soft.

TWO DAYS LATER

The boys say they will be leaving in three days. But today they walked with Wootonekanuske and me and Cedar and Amie and Winnepurket and some of the other children down by the river, hauling along the little ones as well. There we all looked at the signs the animals had left in the fresh snow, and played the old game of seeing how many stories we could read there. We saw the drag-mark of a beaver's fat tail heading straight toward a big cedar he was trying to fell. I thought it might be the same beaver who gave the slap-tail warning and spoiled my aim with the doe. We found an icy slide some playful otters had made on the bank, and nearby we saw the little hand-shaped prints of a raccoon's front paws at the place where she went down to find a break in the ice so she could rinse her food. Then we followed a rabbit's track until we came to the scuffed-up place where a hawk or an owl must have swooped down and caught him, and the tracks ceased. There were a few drops of the rabbit's blood on the snow.

Here is a picture of some of the tracks we saw:

THE NEXT DAY

We young ones took a walk by the river again today. Reading those signs in the snow yesterday made me think of other kinds of reading. I took the chance to ask Wamsutta and Metacom and the others what they knew about this business of those marks the Coat-men make on paper.

Wamsutta said that he knew something about it. He said the Coat-men to the north, the people who call themselves Puritans, have a black-robed powwaw named John Eliot who vows he will teach any of us who wish how to read and write those marks. But we must first agree to give up praying to Manitou and to Squant and all the other Beings who have always been with us, and worship their Beings instead. It seems they really have only one big Being, and then there is somehow a son of his whom they also worship.

Those English must be so lonely, with so few Beings to turn to, and none of them women!

Wamsutta said his father Massasoit will have nothing to do with the matter, though he is always polite to the skinny Eliot, who keeps asking Massasoit's people to come with him and learn to read and to worship the English god. Winnepurket says that lately a number of our people from different villages have heeded the Eliot man. This is especially true of those with very few people left because many of their relatives died off years ago from the spotted sickness. Some have left their own villages to go live together at Natick in what the English call a Praying Town. Winnepurket says that place is all fenced in now, just like Plimoth. There at Natick our own native people are raising English pigs and cattle, and they build big square buildings to shelter the animals. They plant square gardens, and they dress like Coat-men and pray no longer to Manitou and other beings. Instead they pray to that English Father God-and-Son. They do not pray beneath the open sky or before a fire, but inside a square building with a tower atop.

If they do everything the way the Coat-men tell them, then in yet another square building called a schoolhouse they are taught to read the marks on paper and how to make them, too. "But it does not matter!" Wamsutta remarked. "We do not need such writings, and we surely do not need their God!" He spat in the snow, and then he got up and began to pack snowballs and pelt them at an abandoned squirrel's nest.

We were sitting and talking on the riverbank beneath hemlocks. Metacom had been listening to everything his brother and Winnepurket said. All the while, he was drawing quietly with a stick in the snow. This was the shape he kept making: $\wedge$, like a deer's head upside down.

Finally he said softly that he had heard the Eliot person speak, too. He says he has always wondered if there was a way to learn about those marks without having to give up everything that makes us Wampanoags. I startled a little, because that is something I have been thinking about, too.

Metacom told me that if you could read those marks off a paper, you need not be face-to-face with the mark-maker to learn what he or she wished to say. The $\wedge$ sign, he says, is one of their marks. One of the Coat-men who came with Eliot to visit Massasoit taught it to him. It stands for the sound that begins the name of attuks the deer. "Ah, ah, ah!" he said, pointing at that sign he had drawn three times in the snow. He said that if you knew the signs for the rest of the sounds in the name, you could make them side by side, and that group of signs would mean attuks to anyone who read them. Then, he said, if you had a whole paper full of such marks that meant whatever words you wished or promised, maybe no one could doubt a Wampanoag's word, as Coat-men now often do.

But I wonder.

Two days later

Wamsutta and Metacom left us today, along with Massasoit and their kin.

I have been thinking. One thing is plain to me. I do not want iron kettles or glass beads or anything to do with this reading-the-marks business, not if it means living in square Coat-man towns and not being in the care of our Creator and Squant and Mother Corn and all the rest of the Beings who quicken our world.

This is the other thing I have been thinking about the Coat-man's writing. If we do learn it, it might make us lazy, just like Glouskabi's game bag! What if, whenever we wanted a story, we could just reach out and read it from a paper, instead of waiting for the right time and place and the right storyteller to tell it to us?

As it is with us now, when we learn a story, we must hear it again and again, and repeat it to ourselves, until it is in our hearts, and it can never be forgotten.

Also, when we are told a story, we usually hear it when we are gathered together, so it enters into all our hearts at the same time. If we only read the story alone by ourselves, written in Coat-man marks, we would not have to share it, or commit it to memory. It would just be a thing on a paper page that could be burned or trampled and lost, not something that will always live on because it is a part of us as a people.

Here on my birchbark I will make the mark Metacom taught me to make. It is part of the sound of my own name, Weet-ah-moo.

$$\wedge\wedge\wedge\wedge$$

TWO DAYS LATER

Red Hawk the Powwaw says it is time for Cedar and me to go through our special ceremony! It will happen next week, and Red Hawk thinks there will not be very bad weather.

Here is what he has told us will happen. First, there will be a sweat lodge, with the two of us and most of the women of our village and the girls who are old enough.

My Auntie White Frost will lead this ceremony. Then we will be taken off to two separate little wetus in the hills about a mile away from our village, where each of us will fast and pray alone for two days and nights. Our only job will be to keep a fire burning and not let it go out, and to pay attention to all that happens. If things go well, the Powwaw says, we each may have a vision or a dream that will help us to be strong through the rest of our lives.

I thought this time would be mostly about learning hunting skills, but I can tell already it is more about our hearts, and our readiness to be hunters inside ourselves. It is somehow preparing us to be good leaders.

ONE WEEK LATER

It all begins tomorrow.

Squant, please be with us, and please grant us strength. O Squant, and patience!

There will be no drawing on birchbark for these next days. But as always, I will be talking and praying. I will remember everything the Beings may teach me, and perhaps make drawings later.

Today was the sweating ceremony that begins our learning time. Red Hawk and other elders scraped a place clear of snow and built a roaring fire where they heated thirteen stones, one for every moon of the year. They were all the sort of stones that do not explode when they get hot, just like the ones we use for clambakes. When those rocks were glowing with heat the elders carefully fished them out of the burning logs and carried them on big forked sticks into the *pesuponk*, the sweat lodge. This lodge is just like a small wetu, except there is no smoke-hole in the roof and there is nothing inside except a pit dug in the center to hold the rocks. When the lodge was ready, Red Hawk blessed us and left us.

Cedar and I and Mother took off all our clothes and gave them to Nou'gou'mis and another elder, who waited for us outside. Then we squeezed in through the low door. It was very dark, but I could make out Auntie White Frost already sitting inside, waiting for us and praying. There was a clay pot of water beside her and she held a cedar bough in her hand.

When we were all seated in a circle around the pit, Nou'gou'mis, who was guarding the door, closed the flap and sealed us inside. Then my aunt dipped her cedar bough in the pot and shook out droplets of water over the hot stones. They sizzled loudly, and a blast of steam struck us.

Because we were the ones being especially cleansed there, Cedar and I were told to sit in the hottest place, at the back of the lodge. At sweat lodge ceremonies, even when I am sitting near the doorflap, I am never sure I will be able to endure the heat. But I did! Again and again, White Frost sprinkled water from the bough over the pit. Each time water hit the stones, the fresh steam arose and nearly overcame me, and yet I stood it, and so did Cedar.

As always, after a while I started to feel the damp heat purifying me and drawing the uncleanness out of me. I tried to breathe in as deeply as I could, sucking that hot moist air into my lungs. It smelled of clean sweat, and cedar, and the tobacco and other herbs White Frost sometimes offered to the steaming rocks. Once, she must have thrown something like dried mint leaves into the pit, and for a while the whole lodge smelled like a summer meadow.

There were four rounds of prayers, south, west, north, and east, ending in the sunrise direction. With each round we gave thanks to the different spirits of those directions. The elders prayed for me and Cedar. Finally, we were told to ask something for ourselves. Cedar asked that Nou'gou'mis be allowed to live a long time, and keep telling stories. I added my own prayer for Nou'gou'mis silently to hers.

When it came my turn, I asked that our baby sister Snowbird be healed. And then I added, in a whisper, a prayer to all the Beings, to grant me patience.

It must be a heavy burden on Squant to be the only one I have been asking for patience!

When at last we were done, we crawled out of the lodge, one by one. We washed our hot bodies with snow and put on our clothes. I felt relaxed, and yet wide awake. I glanced upward as I tied my moccasins. I have never seen the stars look down so clear and cold.

THE NEXT EVENING

I am in my little wetu on the hill apart from our village, all by myself, sitting and thinking. This is the first night I have ever spent away from my family, not counting sleeping over at Cedar's family's wetu, and that one night I got in late because of skulking back from Plimoth. How I miss my little sister's warm body beside me, and the ordinary sounds of everyone in my family breathing and stirring in the night!

When the Powwaw came to lead me up here after our sweat, Ohkuk started whining and wanted so much to come with me. I hugged my wriggling furry pup, then thrust him right into Wootonekanuske's arms. I whispered that she would have to watch out for him, and for Mother and Snowbird, too, until I returned. She nodded solemnly and held him tight.

I have eaten no food since yesterday noon before the sweat lodge, when we were given corn soup and roasted ground nuts, a hearty feeding before our fast. I have a little pouch of *nokake,* parched and powdered corn, and I can nibble that if I feel the need. But I would like to see how well I can get along on nothing except water.

Fasting is not really hard, except at first. When I missed breakfast today, my stomach growled, and I tried not to think about food. But somehow by now it seems easier.

At first, too, this time alone was very boring, for I have had nothing to work at or play with, and no company, only the tending of my fire. Now I am beginning to feel strangely light and alert. Sometimes I feel a little dreamy. But it is a sharp sort of dreaminess that leaves me aware of things happening around me. When the midday sun melted the snow a little on the boughs of the trees around my wetu, it almost seemed as though I could hear each separate drip.

LATER

I am wrapped in my bearskin, lying in my little wetu.

My only task besides keeping the small fire alight is to be alert to whatever Beings may visit me, or whatever dreams may come to me. I believe my thinking-times have helped to prepare me for these next days. And especially for these nights!

So far, nothing is happening, except for *Ohhomons*, the great horned owl, hooting very loudly in the tall pines outside my wetu.

Hoo-Hoo! HOOO! Hoo-Hoo!

It is a lonesome sound.

I am tending my fire very carefully, not just because it is what I was told to do, but so I will not be cold and alone in the dark.

THE NEXT MORNING

I cannot say if what happened to me last night was vision or dream, but whatever it was, I know it was real.

It seemed to me that I was only lying in my bearskin here in my wetu. I had just checked my little fire, and it looked like it would burn all right for another hour or two, so I could safely try to get a little sleep. But as soon as I started to drop off, I heard a sharp crack outside, as though someone had stepped on a twig, and I lifted open the flap to peer out the doorway. "Who's there?" I called, in as brave a voice as I could muster.

The moon was very bright. There across the clearing from me stood a deer, and I recognized her at once for the very doe Cedar and I had maimed. Even at that distance, I could see the ragged wound in her throat. Her blood gleamed black in the moonlight.

I scrambled out of the wetu and stood up. The doe was gazing at me with her grave and steady eyes. She looked over her shoulder at me, then walked away a few steps and again looked back. It seemed plain she wanted me to follow her. I had brought nothing warm to wrap around me, and here it was the midst of Winter Moon, but it did not seem to matter. Somehow, I did not feel the cold.

Mist was rising off the snow in wide gray ribbons, and sometimes I lost sight of the doe. Once when I could not see her in front of me, I thought I would try to track her, but when I glanced down, I saw that she was leaving no hoofprints in the snow. So I kept forging along. Always, I would find her waiting just ahead for me.

It seemed as if we went on this way for hours. We must have traveled over country that is familiar to me, but everything looked very strange in the snow-mist and the moonlight. Of course, when I think back on it I suppose she was leading me mostly along deer-paths, and not our usual human trails. When at last we broke out of the tattered fog, I was surprised to see that we were standing on the shore, near our seaside village. Could we have come that far so soon, a whole day's journey?

The doe paused and looked back at me, then motioned with her head exactly as if she meant for me to go on in front of her. She stepped delicately to one side, as if to get out of my path. Gingerly, I picked my way by moonlight among the icy rocks. When I got down to the tideline, I saw what I had been brought to see.

There stood a tall woman, with her heavy black hair hanging over her face. I could just make out that with one arm she supported a child on her hip, a child of perhaps one year. The woman stood there as though she were expecting me. I came a step or two closer. Then she drew her thick hair back with her free hand and looked me full in the face, and I saw her square green eyes. That is when I knew it was Squant.

At the same moment I recognized her, I also realized that the child she carried was Snowbird. But such a plump Snowbird! She was laughing and patting Squant's face, and then she squirmed around in her grasp and waved at me.

Squant smiled, too. Then she turned away and walked off among the rocks, carrying my baby sister. I stretched out my arms to her, but neither she nor Snowbird looked back. Somehow I understood I should not follow.

I do not know how I got back to my wetu. Perhaps the doe led me. I do not remember. In any case I awoke, shivering in my bearskin, my cheeks wet with tears. It was close to dawn, and the fire was nearly out. I built it up again, and I am sitting beside it now, thinking on these things.

Oh, Squant, you are as beautiful as all the stories say!

LATER

I do not know whether what I saw last night means that Squant will heal Snowbird, or if it means she will die and Squant will help her spirit to go where it must go. That is all left up to Manitou to decide.

Whether it be life or death, I know one thing in my heart from what happened last night, and that is how tenderly our people are cared for. We are in the hands of all the Beings.

Tonight will be the second and last night of my fast. Perhaps there are more things to be shown to me, perhaps not. I feel a little weak and light-headed, but I am still well able to tend the fire. After all, the Powwaw said that is all that is asked of me. I feed it little curls of cedar bark when it threatens to go out, and I talk to it as I build it up, coaxing it aflame. It is a living being, and it is my friend.

THE NEXT MORNING

The doe came to me again last night. Again I was lying wrapped in my bearskin, tending my fire, but on this second night I was fully awake and waiting.

Sometime in the deep night I heard the sort of soft

snorting and pawing noises that deer make when they are nervous and want to be gone from a place. I opened the flap, and there the doe stood, as before. This time there was no swirling ground-mist, only the moonlight. I walked forward to meet her, and again she led me along the trails of her deer-people through the forest.

This seemed to me a far longer walk than last night's. Once, when we crested a hill, I spied what looked like a great fire down in the valley below us. It lit up the sky, and I thought I could faintly hear Coat-men shouting and the war cries of our people, but the doe did not halt, and soon the light and the noises faded behind us. It was strange, because I knew more or less where I was, and there is no Coat-man village near there.

We walked long enough so that it became dawn, and then full daylight. The air grew softer, and I could see new leaves on the trees. Had we walked not only for a night, but through whole moons, I wondered? Had we walked into spring?

At last the doe paused when we came to a certain clearing. She did not motion for me to go ahead, and so we stood side by side, she and I, looking at the scene before us.

In that clearing it was indeed a spring morning. I guessed it was probably *Namassack Keeswush*, Time of Catching Fish, because the white sprays of shadbush were blooming. When those shrubs flower, they are telling us it is time for the big spring runs of fish coming upriver to spawn. Close by I could hear the earth-shaking rumble of one of our fish-catching waterfall places. That noise of thundering water filled my ears and came straight up through the soles of my feet, so it possessed my whole body.

I thought we must be at Peskeompskut, Exploding Rocks, though that waterfall is a full two days' journey and more from Nemasket, and I did not see how the doe and I could have walked there so quickly.

All at once into that springtime clearing with the light sifting down through the new green leaves, two women and two men came and sat down. As strange as it seems, I could tell right away I was looking at Wootonekanuske, Metacom, and myself, but we were all three full-grown. The grown-up me had a baby in a cradleboard on my back, and a handsome boy of nine or so worked at stringing a bow at Wootonekanuske's feet. The other man with us was very handsome, and he seemed to know us well. But I did not know him, and the first thing I thought was, Where is Wamsutta? Shouldn't he be the fourth one here? All four of us looked very solemn and weary.

There was a patch of bloodroot with its white flower cups and red stems growing beside the log where Metacom sat. He reached down to pick some, and the red juice stained his hand. I thought he must be going to smear it on his arms and face, as we usually do to repel mosquitoes, but instead he did a strange thing. He crushed the bloodroot stems and rubbed his thumb well in the bright juice, and he marked his own forehead with a single line of red. Then he stood and did the same with the brows of the grown-up me and the baby I carried and the strange man. But Wootonekanuske and her boy he did not mark. What this means, I do not know.

As before, I woke in my little wetu, not remembering how I got there. It was still nighttime, still deepest winter. My fire had almost gone out, and I hurried to add wood and blow it aflame. Now though I am trembling with the strangeness of it all, there is a heavy sleepiness coming on me.

Later

Red Hawk has come to pray with me and take me back to my parents. I will finish my thinking later.

That evening

I still do not know what the dream or vision of last night means, any more than I know what my sighting of Squant meant. Before I was allowed to go home, Red Hawk made me sit down with him by my fire and tell him everything that happened to me while I was fasting.

The Powwaw asked me a lot of questions:

> Did the doe address you by name?
>
> In which direction did the Squant Being walk when she left carrying your sister?
>
> How old did you and your sister look to be when you saw yourselves in the clearing?

I could answer some of his questions, but not all of them.

After he finished asking me about what I had seen, he sat for a long time in silence. At last he said that all I had seen was important, but no one could say whether these things were truly in the time-to-be or only shadows of what might possibly come to pass. He sighed deeply. Then he said that both Cedar and I had seen things that seemed to speak of bitter wars. I long to know what Cedar saw.

But what of the first night, I asked, the sight of Squant,

with Snowbird in her arms? Does it mean my baby sister will live or die?

Red Hawk smiled. Either way, he said, you know already that she is cherished. I nodded, and hung my head. I did know that. But I had so wished to hear the Powwaw say, Oh, that certainly means she will be cured!

Red Hawk said that I was now opening wider to the spirit world, and that I must now begin to pay more attention than ever before to my dreams.

Red Hawk stood up. It was a sparkling winter day. A cardinal whistled over our heads <u>cheer-cheer-cheer.</u> He glowed bright red against the snowy branches. His greenish-brown wife bustled about on the ground, under the cover of bushes. I suppose she waited for him to tell her it was safe to come out.

Inside the wetu my fire was still burning, and the Powwaw said what a good job I had done of keeping it alight these last two days and nights. He added, "That is mostly what it is all about, daughter, about keeping the fire alive." Then he carefully scraped up the ashes and told me to put some in my special medicine pouch before we started back to our village.

That Afternoon

Home again.

I did not feel as though I was supposed to ask Red Hawk what he meant about the fire. But I did ask him if it would be wrong to speak to anyone else of what happened to me during my fast. He said that was up to me.

As I trudged behind him toward home, I began to cry quietly. I suppose I cried for weariness and relief. But I think I was also crying for that carefree, foolish girl I was only last summer, the Weetamoo who had little thought of death and dreams and destiny, except to imagine how fine it would be to be a sachem, with no ordinary chores and no one to tell her what to do.

Late that Night

It is so sweet to hear my family breathing in their sleep around me, to feel my little sister beside me and Ohkuk curled up at my feet, to smell the home smells of a banked fire and corn soup and damp dog and warm bodies, to hear Snowbird cry softly in the dark out of her dreaming. It is as though I never left.

And yet I did, and I know I will never be the same.

The elders held another sweat tonight, to mark Cedar's and my return from our fasting vigils. Again, we were seated besides each other, but of course there was no chance for us to speak together. Her face looked so different from the usual face of my smiling friend. There was a new glow and a new seriousness about her. She looked older.

I think perhaps I must, too.

I think if I speak to anyone of what I saw, it must be Cedar.

Again, I wonder what she saw, and if she will want to tell me.

THE NEXT MORNING

A streaky pink dawn, and with it came the daily chores, scooping up snow for water, fetching in the day's firewood, building up the fire, setting the cooking-pot aboil. I slept soundly last night. But I do remember the last thought I had before I went to sleep. It was this: Why was Wamsutta not in that clearing with us?

Dream or vision, whatever it was, it made me realize how much I would miss him if he were not there in my future, if the future is indeed what the doe led me to see.

He is sometimes very arrogant and boastful, but he is also strong and brave, and he makes me feel very alive, somehow.

Perhaps I saw a glimpse of the future in which he was simply off hunting, or on some other errand.

SQUOCHEEKEESWUSH
WHEN THE SUN HAS STRENGTH TO THAW
[FEBRUARY 1654]

I spoke with Cedar for the first time today since our fasting days. It was raw, angry weather, with wind whipping in our faces. She and I were both supposed to be out fetching wood, but we knew no one would miss us if we took half an hour for a walk by the river.

I told her that Red Hawk said I might speak of what happened to me during the fast if I wished. She said he told her the same. But then she did not offer to tell me anything! She just looked down at her feet.

"Please, Cedar," I said, "I must share this with someone."

"All right," she agreed, and so I went on to tell her what happened on the first night of my fast. Her eyes got wide as I went on with my tale.

"So you have seen Squant," she said softly, after I finished the story of that first night, the story of seeing Squant and Snowbird. "That is a very great thing."

Then she told me about the many times she has quietly slipped away from her family and her chores and roamed the shore, half-hoping to come upon Squant. But all she has ever seen is a slender shaft of light striking a tide pool, and the long strands of kelp rippling in the current so beautifully, it might almost be a woman's hair.

I have seen those things, too, among the rocks and the water, and had the same thought: that it is like catching a glimpse of Squant. Here is a picture of the kelp and the rock it is anchored to:

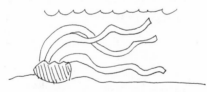

There was no time for more talk, but we have agreed to meet every morning and hear each other's stories of our fasting-time.

The next day

Today Cedar and I went wood-gathering again. It makes me think, how would we ever get to gossip and trade stories if we did not have outside chores? This morning I got the chance to tell my friend more about what happened.

When I came to the story of the second night, Cedar listened even more intently. "Oh, Weetamoo," she said when I was done, and she grabbed my hand. Her own hand was trembling. "I am very much afraid!"

We promised to meet tomorrow at the woodpile, and to walk out together again.

I came home to our longhouse, and when my chores were done I went back to beading the deerskin sash. It is nearly done, and I think quite the best piece of beadwork I have ever made. Wootonekanuske thinks so, too. She ran her finger gently over the pattern. "It looks like waves," she whispered, and I knew then that I had beaded it well.

Late that night

I know Wootonekanuske wants very much to ask me about what happened during my fasting-time. I often catch her watching me with her curious bright eyes from across the fire. But she holds back, and I am glad, for I think it is all too much to tell her now while she is still so young, especially the part about us being grown and sad, and her with her little son.

THE NEXT DAY

It is miserable weather still, so cold and wet that my chin and nose are chapped. But Cedar and I went walking out, anyway. This time, she did most of the talking.

Cedar said that in all her two days of fasting she never left her wetu and her little fire in the way I seemed to, nor did our wounded doe come to seek her out. Instead, a blue jay hung around her the whole time she was camped there. He was a saucy, friendly fellow who jabbered in his screechy language at her. She thought perhaps he was her spirit-helper, and she said Red Hawk told her later that was probably right. Spirit-helpers do not need to be big animals, after all, he explained. She was grateful to the blue jay, because she needed help and company.

What poor Cedar endured was not journeys but dreams, and they were terrible dreams! She says the dreams were mostly just pictures, one after another, pictures of villages set on fire. Some were Coat-man villages, some were the villages of our own people. On and on they rolled, these fiery scenes, until she tells me she was terrified to sleep.

I thought about the fire I had glimpsed in the distance while the doe and I went on our long walk on my second night of fasting.

But twice, Cedar said, she dreamed other dreams, dreams that were more like stories. Today she told me about one of them.

In her dream she, too, found herself at Peskeompskut, Exploding Rocks, the same waterfall-place where I thought I had traveled. In her dream, too, the season looked to be Namassack Keeswush, the Time of Catching Fish.

It seemed she was just at an ordinary fish-camp, doing ordinary fish-camp chores. But when she went to fill a pot from the river below the falls and drew it out, the water was red with blood. At first she thought it must only be the blood of gutted salmon or alewives or some other fish. But then, as she looked up, that whole river was choked with the bodies of our people, women and elders and children alike. When she turned away from the river and looked at the bank, she could see that all the camp wetus and fish-drying racks lay broken and scattered and set ablaze. Even over the noise of the falls she could hear loud weeping and lamenting.

"Lost, lost, lost!" a woman's voice was crying.

She awoke in her little fasting-wetu to the blue jay jeering cheerfully at her. It was once again a winter morning, and there was brilliant sunlight on the snow. But she said she could not put aside that dream of a beautiful river in springtime running red with blood.

We were both quiet for a long while after that. At last I said that I thought perhaps we had seen parts of the same terrible thing, she in one way, and I in another. She nodded, and said she thought so, too. Our heads were bent to keep the chill wind out of our faces. But it was not only the wind that brought tears to our eyes.

I used to think that this fasting-time would be all about becoming splendid hunters and warriors and councillors, but I can see now that I was wrong. Cedar agrees. It seems to be more about us learning sorrow, she says.

Yes, I say.

But then I think of seeing Squant. And I think of what the Powwaw told me as he and I started home from the hill. I can still hear his voice in my ears:

"That is mostly what it is all about, daughter, about keeping the fire alive."

I told Cedar when I saw her today while we were gathering wood what Red Hawk had said to me about the fire. I asked her what she supposed it meant. She thought a long time. Then she said, it must be about keeping our lives going, do you not think?

"I think so," I said. "And maybe not just our two small lives, but our people's lives, or maybe our way of life?"

"Yes," Cedar said. "And I suppose," she added thoughtfully, "as with keeping a campfire going, this person and that one will often have different ideas about how best to do so."

I looked hard at her, but she would not meet my eyes. She still kept her chin tucked down, though the wind had slacked off at last.

"I only mean like your father Corbitant and Massasoit," Cedar said, "and how differently they feel about being friendly with the Coat-men. Or your father and my father, and how differently they think about turning out those many strings of wampum for the Coat-men's use." She scuffed the toe of her moccasin in the snow.

I understood what she meant. It is going to be hard to decide what will be best for our people when we become sachems. Only a few moons ago, when I thought about becoming a sachem, I mostly imagined advising people and never having to do chores. But keeping the fire going will mean much more than that.

We were very near the place where Metacom had drawn the first sign for attuks the deer, $\wedge$ for the sound of *Ah*, over and over in the snow. I remembered how that $\wedge$ also means the sound for the middle part of my own name, Weet-*ah*-moo. With the toe of my own moccasin, I tried making that sign in the snow.

THAT NIGHT

I just remembered that Cedar never told me her second whole dream. I must ask her tomorrow.

There is hard sleet beating against the bark that covers our longhouse. Wootonekanuske is snoring lightly. Somehow that sound does not annoy me much these days, not since my fasting-time.

After last night's ice storm, the whole forest is glittering. As it warms up a little, the ice cracks off the branches and drops to the ground and astounds Ohkuk.

When I asked Cedar about her other dream, she seemed reluctant. But finally she said, "It was about you and me, Weetamoo."

Then she wanted to tell me no more, but I insisted. I said it was not fair to let me know there was a dream with us both in it, and then to keep it from me.

"All right," she said finally. She told me that in her dream we both seemed to be grown sachems. We were standing on either side of a stream, the little stream that feeds the Big Swamp that lies between our two seaside villages. She said I was grandly dressed, and painted for war, with much fine jewelry hung about me. I stretched my hands out to her across the stream and asked her to come join with me and my brother-in-law Metacom in a great fight against the Coat-men! But she felt afraid and said she would not join with me, nor should her people, either.

At that, she said, I dropped my arms to my sides, and with a proud look I turned on my heel and vanished among the dense trees of the Big Swamp.

I asked her if she thought that meant there would

come a time when we truly would not be friends. We have spent our girlhood imagining just how it will be when we are sachems together!

She only shook her head and said she did not know.

It is so hard to know if these sightings and dreams are true visions of what will be, or only warnings of what might be.

One thing also troubles me: Where was Wamsutta in Cedar's dream? Why was it only Metacom and I who proposed war?

TWO DAYS LATER

There is to be a great deer hunt, and Cedar and I are to be included! We will travel to the east of here, even farther inland, where the deer have mostly gone, avoiding the Coat-men. Some of the other women will be coming along to butcher and cure and help pack the meat back to our village, but Cedar and I will be allowed to be among the hunters, even if we do not do any of the actual shooting.

Mother will not be coming with us. She and Wootonekanuske and Snowbird will stay behind. It is a long journey, much too long for Snowbird, as frail as she seems now. But we will bring back fresh deer meat, and then we can make venison broth to help her grow strong!

It has been a two day's journey to the deer-hunting place. The snow is deep and firmly packed, and we can snowshoe atop it easily.

When we came to the deer-hunting place, I could see how what my father said was true about making good territory for the deer by burning away the undergrowth. Here the trees are widely spaced, and there is no tangle of brush beneath them, but there is an abundance of dried grass poking out of the snow. Moss and lichens, the food the deer love best, grow thickly on the tree trunks. The deer have good browsing grounds, and the deer hunters can spy them easily in the openings between trees.

Then there is another thing to help hunters. Whoever burned the brush left two long lines of hedges that stretch farther than my eye can see. They fan out widely, like the shape a flock of geese forms when they fly: $\vee$. We have made camp near where the two lines almost come together, and here my father and the other elders called us younger ones into council.

At this time of the year, they reminded us, the Deer People like to be together, so probably we will find quite a few of them all gathered near one another. Tomorrow, some of us will stay here near the narrow opening in the hedge-fence with bows and arrows. Others will go out to the wide mouth of the hedges, and drive the deer in this direction. Then when the deer crowd toward the opening, the hunting should be easy and plentiful.

Cedar and I are not to be bowhunters this time. We are to be among the drivers, shooing the deer in the direction of the hunters.

After the elders set forth their plans and assigned us all our jobs, we prayed for a long time. We gave thanks to Manitou for making the Deer People in the first place, and we spoke to the deer themselves, asking that they yield up their lives bravely and with grace. We offered up the smoke of tobacco and other herbs, and we pledged to kill the deer as quickly and cleanly as we might. I stole a glance over at Cedar. I could see that she, too, was feeling ashamed all over again about how thoughtlessly the two of us had set off a-hunting on that autumn morning three moons ago.

The next evening

The hunt was most successful! Cedar and I and the other drivers spread out and slowly stalked the deer. We herded them between the lines of hedges until they funneled right down to the narrow place where the hunters awaited them with bows and arrows and spears. This is a good way to hunt, because the deer come so close, the hunters can judge which will be the best deer to take. That way they can avoid killing the does who are young enough to give birth to fawns — as Cedar's and my doe, alas, was — or any deer who seems unwell.

At first I was disappointed not to be on the bow-and-arrow end of things, but I was so honored to walk side by side with the others in a thin line and stalk the deer over the crisp snow. How beautiful they are, the Deer People! It is important to take only as many of their lives as will be needed to sustain ours, and to give them all the thanks and honor they deserve in return.

We traveled here with only pouches of nokake, our parched corn flour, to eat, but tonight in camp we will feast well before starting back to Nemasket tomorrow. Already, before we begin roasting the haunches of venison, my father and Red Hawk are throwing bits of trimmed fat on the fire and offering the delicious smoke up to the Creator.

I should feel happy. Here I am, on my first big hunting trip. Today I did my stalking job well, and I am looking forward to the venison we will be eating tonight, and the stories we shall probably hear around the fire.

But there is some heaviness on my heart. I cannot say what it is. It is like the heaviness you feel in the summer on a sweltering day when there will be a big thunderstorm later that afternoon.

Later this night

Tonight Red Hawk told us the story of how Winter once took possession of all the land and made life very hard for our people. Enormous sheets of ice covered our beautiful earth. It was so cold in those times that even the cooking pots hung over the fires froze solid. But finally Spring conquered Winter, and when his whole world began to melt, old Winter had to flee far up to the northlands. Now he comes only once a year for a few moons, and he is mostly milder than he was when he had his full powers.

It is one of my favorite stories, but somehow Red Hawk is not as good a storyteller as Nou'gou'mis, or that Abnaki man who visited us at midwinter. He is a better powwaw than a teller of tales, I think! But perhaps my mind was not fully on the story, as it should have been.

Tomorrow we start for home. We will move more slowly on this return journey, as we will be burdened with our packs of meat and skins.

THREE DAYS LATER
NEMASKET

O, Squant, my baby sister is gone!

A WEEK LATER

O Squant, please grant me and my family peace in our hearts.

The hardest grieving falls to my poor mother and Wootonekanuske. There were few people here at Nemasket when Snowbird died because so many of us were away on the deer hunt. There came a long terrible night when the baby became more and more blue-faced and fought for breath, and my mother and sister had no one to help them except Loon Woman, who crooned soothing songs in her strange voice. They could do nothing except hold her and watch her slip away. Then my mother and Wootonekanuske wept in Loon Woman's thin arms.

We have blackened our faces with soot, and we gathered together to mourn her. Everyone filed through our longhouse, and stroked our cheeks, and whispered *kutchimmoke*, and *noowantamone*. Now we may no longer speak her name, for fear it would call her back. We must say instead words like *The Baby*, or *She Who Was Once Here*.

My father and others hacked into the frozen earth to make her grave. We buried my sister in her little doeskin dress, curled up on her side as though she still lay within our mother's womb, and we wrapped her in woven cattail mats. I put my beaded sash into the grave with her. Cedar and her family brought child-sized vessels of parched corn and dried meat for the Baby's long journey to the southwest, where the dead dwell. There in that place, they say, rejoicing and feasting and love never end.

When I first had the idea for the bead design, and declared I would make it for something special, I never thought its destiny would be to travel with my baby sister to that far land. Perhaps there she will become some other family's baby.

Be with her, Squant. I keep remembering how that night on the shore I saw her whole and healthy and laughing in your arms.

O Squant, please, be with our mother.

Wootonekanuske cried mightily, and lay awake for several nights after the burial. I held her and comforted her. How terrible that she should have to stare into the face of our sister's death! But she is young, and she is springing back. Today for the first time we took Ohkuk down by the river and threw sticks for him to chase. He has been mourning like the rest of us, and whimpering in the night. But today there was strong sunlight, and the snow was melting off the branches. I think Winter will probably be driven back up north again pretty soon, just as in the old story.

But our mother does not do well. She barely eats anything, and she has no energy. She speaks in the lowest of voices, when she speaks at all, and often stares vacantly at the air. Wootonekanuske and I try to be with her and help her as much as we can, but I think she needs some stronger medicine.

I have thought of telling her about my sighting of Squant and our baby sister, but I do not know if that is the right thing to do.

This moon I am almost as old as my mother was when she married my father. Two winters from now, I will be as old as she was when she gave birth to me. This is frightening to me. Not so long ago I would boast that I was old enough and smart enough to do anything. Now I am not so sure, not at all.

WAPICUMMILCUM
WHEN ICE IN THE RIVER IS GONE
[EARLY MARCH]

Despite our name for this moon, the ice is not yet all gone from the river!

How I long for spring and the return of the birds who flew south last fall! Maybe they will be coming back from so far to the south and west, they will have caught a glimpse of The One Who Went Away on her long journey. I am drawing how the *honckock*, the geese, look when they are flying home to us:

Two days later

This is the time of year when we all long so much for the fresh greens of spring instead of the dried corn and meat and berries we live on through most of the winter. We are grateful for all of our food, of course, but right now my appetite craves the new shoots of pokeweed and dandelion and cattail, and the baby fiddlehead ferns. Oh, for some watercress, or the clean, sharp taste of wild onion on my tongue!

Here is a picture of the curled fiddlehead fern-tops I am especially hungry for. They look like green eagle claws!

I keep thinking some fresh spring greens would help Mother recover, too.

The powwaw Red Hawk has suggested it might be good to have a ceremony for Mother, as she is still so sunk in grief for The One Who Went Away.

Two days later

Wootonekanuske and I went foraging this morning and found the first bright green cattail shoots coming up in the swamp by the river, that same swamp where Cedar and I tried so clumsily to track the wounded doe. We fetched the cattail shoots home and peeled them, and I am slipping them into the stewpot. I will fish them out before they are too well done, and we will see if Mother likes their fresh crunchiness.

That night

Mother did eat the cattail shoots, and a spoonful or two of broth from the venison stew besides. After she ate she drew me and Wootonekanuske close and hugged us, and said she was so grateful to have us two good daughters beside her. But then she started to cry again.

Red Hawk is going to hold a sweat for Mother and all our women family and friends tomorrow.

I wish you could come to her, Squant — I do not mean that you should appear to her, but it would be wonderful if you could just somehow come into her heart.

I believe Mother worries that The One Who Went Away is wandering alone and lost between worlds, and I know that is not true.

TWO DAYS LATER

I think the sweat has done Mother good, and I have more wonderful news besides!

Mother slept more easily last night than I have seen her sleep since The One Who Used to Be Here left us. While we were shut up in the heat of the pesuponk, she wept hard and sweated a great deal. Each time the vessel of water was passed around for us to drink from, she drank more than the rest of us, and sweated it right back out again, or so it seemed to me. I think her body got rid of a great deal of grief last night in that way, and this is good, for too much grief poisons a person.

We all wailed and prayed for The One Who Went Away. When it came my turn, in my prayer I said that I knew my baby sister was safe. Then I told about how I had seen her in Squant's arms. It was dark in the pesuponk, but Wootonekanuske and I were crammed in on either side of Mother, and I could feel her whole body at first stiffen and then slowly relax as I spoke.

Oh, how I wish I had talked to Mother about this before. But I think she was not ready to hear any words of comfort until now.

When we emerged from the heat of the sweat lodge, Mother said she did not want to risk the cold shock of coming straight from the steam into the snow-washing. Wootonekanuske and I asked why, and she lifted one of my hands and one of my sister's and held both of them flat against her brown belly. "Another one is coming," she whispered.

So there is to be a new baby in our cradleboard, come *Taquontikeeswush*, the Harvest Moon!

Mother did not have any babies for a long time in between Wootonekanuske and The One Who Went Away. Losing this last child for whom she waited so long shook her very hard.

Dear Squant, please help this new Forming Person to be sound and healthy.

A WEEK LATER

The snow is almost all melted now, and the black-masked honckock are trailing in their great arrowhead-shaped flights overhead. It is gloriously muddy! Ohkuk skids around in that mud, and he yips every time his paws slip out from under him. Mother is eating and sleeping well now, and I feel hopeful that all will yet be well.

But I am still haunted by the strange and solemn things Cedar and I were shown during our fasting-time.

I think often of those boys, Wamsutta and Metacom, back there at their seaside village. In just a week or two we will travel to one of the fishing camps to net and trap the fish swimming upriver to spawn. Then it will be time for us to fold up our mats and pack up our household goods to move back to our own seaside village on the bay, and begin planting our fields with the three sisters, corn and bean and squash. So I am sure we shall see those boys again, perhaps at the fishing-camp, but certainly during the summer.

So much has happened since the last days we were all together. I have been through fasting and visions and hunting and death, and I scarcely know how I can speak to Wamsutta and Metacom of it all.

Cedar and her family have already returned to the shore to get a head start on collecting shells for their wampum-making. They left yesterday, and I wept to see her go. I am weeping still. She is the only one who shares all that has happened to me during this past *Papone,* this last hard winter.

I pray that Cedar's dream is wrong, the one about us being divided from each other.

THE NEXT DAY

Yesterday afternoon when I was crying about Cedar's departure, and all that has happened to make our lives different and strange, I suddenly noticed a soft crooning coming from the corner of the longhouse. It was Loon Woman, and she was gesturing to me as well as she could to come nearer to her. We two were alone, for once, except for Seal and Gull, who napped on their bearskin. I thought I was crying very quietly, but she must have heard me in her heart, somehow. I crept over and laid my head on her lap, and she stroked my hair with her little bird-claw hand. Then the tears came freely. It shames me to think how such a short time ago Wootonekanuske and I feared her.

Two days later

Father is making another journey to Plimoth tomorrow to talk about who should be in charge of what land, and how to contain the Coat-men's pigs and cows. This time he tells me I am to go with him!

But he says on no account am I to go inside the gates of their settlement. Father and all the other elders still think it is not safe for any of us Wampanoag women and girls to go among the Coat-men. Father says they have far less respect for women than our people do. Bad things have happened; some of our women have been attacked and dishonored, not at Plimoth, but among other Coat-man settlements to the north.

I will do as Father says, and not step inside the gates. But at least I will make the trip with him, and wait just outside their fence, and when Father has something to report he will come out and consult with his trusted councillors and me.

When he told me this, he raised an eyebrow at me and said, "Well, Daughter, maybe it will be a more comfortable trip for you this time, since you can just walk along the trail in plain sight behind me, and not go groveling along in the middle of the blackberries and poison ivy and sumac!"

THE NEXT AFTERNOON
PLIMOTH

Here we are at Plimoth.

Once again my father, Corbitant, has disappeared between the wide gates of the Coat-men, and once again I am planning on skulking beside their palisade of saplings, just as I did last autumn, at Harvest Moon.

It is a very wet spring so far, and the mosquitoes are already thick. The blackflies will be coming upon us soon.

On our way here from Nemasket, I spied the first early patch of bloodroot I have seen this spring. Such clear white cups of flowers, and such bright red stems! I picked some, and wrapped them with green dandelion leaves, and tucked them carefully in my pouch. Inside that pouch there still lies the fragrant sprig of rosemary the Coat-woman gave me last fall. I hope to pay her back today.

Here is a picture of the bloodroot:

THAT SAME NIGHT

We are camped outside the gates of Plimoth. I am guessing that nothing much came of Father's meeting. At any rate, he is grumpy and chooses not to speak to any of us about it.

While I was waiting for my father this afternoon, I crept up to the same Coat-person fence I peeked through before. Sure enough, I saw that same nice old Coat-woman. She was wearing her bulky Coat-women clothes and slapping at mosquitoes, and trying all the while to plant her garden. She had kernels of Mother Corn in hand. In a dish she had seeds of Sister Squash, and other seeds I did not recognize.

I peered for a time through the hole in the fence, and after a while I rattled the palings a little. I just knew that Coat-woman would hear me, and she did. She grinned widely and came waddling over to the fence. "Ho, Little Savage!" she said, and reached her pink fingers through the gap in the paling to touch my brown ones.

I beckoned to her to put her eye to the gap in the fence. Then I pointed to the cloud of mosquitoes and made as if to slap at them. At last, I pulled the bloodroot from my pouch. I squeezed a stem and smeared a little of the bright red juice on my own face and arms, and smiled. The Coat-woman looked at me with such intelligent eyes, I could tell she understood me perfectly. I thought suddenly of Loon Woman, who also does not need words to know things. Then I thrust my fistful of bloodroot through the gap in the fence, and she took it from me.

"Thank you, Little Savage," she said.

I know those Coat-man words.

They are the same as our *taubotneanawayean*, I thank you.

So now, there you have it! I have touched hands with a Coat-woman, and traded one of our plants for one of hers.

Perhaps Father's dealings did not go well, but I feel good about mine.

I was glad to give the Coat-woman bloodroot to fend off the biting insects. But it made me remember my sight of a grown Metacom smearing that juice across our foreheads, not in a manner to repel bugs, but in a way somehow to mark us apart.

I think we were being marked for death.

But if that is so, might it mean that Wootonekanuske and her son, whom he did not mark, shall live?

NAMASSACK KEESWUSH
TIME OF CATCHING FISH
[EARLY APRIL]
NEMASKET

Now is the time we travel together to the fish-camps, to trap the fish that fill the rivers in their eagerness to swim upstream to spawn. It is best to try to catch them just below a waterfall, where they gather and must try to leap it. There we can easily spear them or sometimes even scoop them out by the basketful. We smoke most of them on drying racks on the riverbank to preserve them for year-round eating. But in fish-camp, we also broil them fresh. How I love to take a broiled shad in my bare hands, and strip the sweet flesh from its spiny backbone!

There are many places where we can go to do this spring fishing, but this year Father has decided it will be Peskeompskut, Exploding Rocks, the very place that was in Cedar's and my fasting-time visions and dreams. It seems as though everyone will be gathering there this year, since the fish-run was reported at our winter gathering to be so good last year. They will be so thick, Father predicts, we will almost be able to walk across the river on their slippery silver backs! I know Cedar and her family will be coming, and I am thinking that Massasoit and those boys might well be there, too.

THE NEXT DAY
PESKEOMPSKUT

It is true, just as I hoped! Everyone seems to have selected Peskeompskut as this spring's fish-run place to gather. We are all here, me and Wootonekanuske, Cedar, even Wamsutta and Metacom, and their little sister Amie. But there is scarcely time to talk with one another, what with making camp, and assembling the fish-drying racks, and setting up the weirs. The fish teem in the river, and they try so bravely to overleap the thundering falls. It is all gleaming silver sides and fins, gaping mouths and flashing tails and fish-smelling spray in our faces!

Here is a picture of one of the salmon:

THREE DAYS LATER

I took a little time by myself today to walk downriver around the bend from our fishing-camp. I came upon the very clearing I visited with the doe in my fasting-time. The shadbush is blooming, just as it was in my fasting-time walk. But in that vision, I was grown, and today I am not, at least not yet.

I do not know what to make of any of this.

I think much about what I saw during my fast, and how, of the two boys, only Metacom was in my dream.

Metacom is a thoughtful, brave person. But somehow he does not cause me to feel both shy and alive the way Wamsutta does. I can see the way Wootonekanuske looks at Metacom with such admiration, and I think it is no accident that he always wears the woven belt she gave him. Metacom could never be my husband. But maybe he will indeed be my brother-in-law someday. I would be very glad of that.

Wootonekanuske and Metacom are very young, but I think they already know each other's hearts.

And I think I know mine.

I hope I get a chance to speak with Wamsutta. So far here at Peskeompskut, I have only seen him at a distance.

He is just as arrogant and cocky as ever. But what a proud way he has of walking, and how handsome his uplifted chin, and how his dark eyes flash!

THE NEXT DAY

I met Wamsutta downstream from Peskeompskut. Well, to tell the truth, I did not exactly meet him. I more or less followed him.

"What are you looking for, little Pocasset girl?" he said, turning around to meet me.

I said that I was certainly not looking for anything he could give me, but I think he knew right away that I did not mean that. He reached out and touched my cheek very gently.

"Nothing? Are you sure of that?" he asked. I scarcely know how it happened, but suddenly we were in each other's arms.

Once he was holding me close, it seemed as if my tongue would not stop talking. When I told him about my baby sister's death, he wiped my tears away. I spoke about the Forming Child we expect in the Harvest Moon. He said he was very happy for our family. Somehow, I went on to tell him that I thought he was a very careless and boastful person. By then I was laughing and crying at the same time. He just kept looking down and grinning at me. Finally I said that I supposed I loved him.

But I did not tell him how, during my fasting-time, I could not see him in the future.

By the time we walked back to the fishing-camp together, I think we both knew we would someday be married. Someday — not just yet. There is all the business of Wamsutta getting someone trusted to come and speak to my parents. If our elders agree, they must go about putting together a suitable amount of wampum and furs and household goods for a marriage.

But I know it is this arrogant, teasing, kind, and thoughtful person whom I love.

THE NEXT DAY

Our family is heading back to Nemasket, and then right away we will be setting out for Mettapoiset, our seaside village. My heart feels so full. I am longing for the clamming and the swimming, and even the corn-planting. We cannot set the corn in the earth until the oak-leaves are at least as big as a mouse's ear, but that will probably be in less than a week!

I miss Wamsutta, but there will be so much to do in these next weeks, it scarcely matters.

One week later
Mettapoiset

At last we are back at Mettapoiset. How good it feels to wade in the cold salt bay once more! Ohkuk races along the shore and barks at the seagulls, tossing up sand with his big clumsy paws. The gulls just fly twenty paces off and land again and yawp and look back at him with disdain.

The next day

Tomorrow will be the day we plant Mother Corn and her sisters, the beans and the pumpkins. There has been plenty of discussion in our village, as there always is every year, over whether the white-oak leaves are or are not yet as big as a mouse's ear. But my mother and Auntie White Frost and others consulted Loon Woman and

Nou'gou'mis, and they all agreed that it was indeed time to plant, so that settles it!

This timing is a delicate matter, though, because all three Sister crops can bruise easily when they are little, and we want to make sure we are beyond the nights of the last late frosts. Also, it is important to plant corn while the moon is full, so its growing power can help pull our baby seedlings up out of the soil.

The full moon will be in two days.

The next day

I used to complain about doing the ordinary woman's chore of planting, of clearing the ground and bending over with my digging stick and poking holes in the ground, of lugging my sacks of the separate seeds all over the fields.

This spring, I do not feel that way. It was such a good feeling to be planting the Sisters in the warm earth. Mother was, of course, out in the field with us. Already her belly is swelling a little.

All the while I was planting the seed, I was thinking ahead four moons, when it will be late summer and we will be eating the delicious roasted Mother Corn. And then in six moons, our new Forming Person will join us.

In time, I think Wamsutta and I will be husband and wife, sachems helping our two bands, and perhaps we will have children of our own.

Who knows what will happen beyond that? I fear some of the things I have been given to see — warfare and burning, and a world without Wamsutta, a time when he and I will both make that long journey to the southwest, the land of the dead.

But that is only a journey all of us must make, sooner or later.

Wamsutta says the Coat-men believe that when they die, they will be snatched up into the sky. Perhaps that is right for them.

Planting corn, and giving birth. Ruling our people well. I was thinking about all those things today as I poked the dried-up seeds in the earth.

Dear Squant, I think it is all part of the same business.
It is about keeping the fire going.

EPILOGUE

Wamsutta, as it turns out, did not become Weetamoo's first husband. She was briefly married to Winnepurket, the sachem of Saugus, who died soon after their marriage. But just as Weetamoo foresees, she married Wamsutta, and her sister Wootonekanuske married Metacom, probably during their late teenage years. These double marriages strengthened the ties between their two bands of Wampanoag people, the Pocasset and the Pokanoket.

When Massasoit, a great leader among the Wampanoag nation, died in 1661, his older son Wamsutta inherited his sachemship. The exact date of Corbitant's death was not recorded, but Weetamoo eventually succeeded her father as sachem of the Pocassets. A woman named Awashonks, the historical person upon whom the character of Cedar is based, also became sachem of her people, the Sakonnets.

Soon after Massasoit's death, Wamsutta and Metacom traveled to Plimoth, where they asked the authorities to give them English names. The English decided to call Wamsutta Alexander, after the great Greek warrior-king Alexander the Great. They named Metacom after Philip of Macedonia, Alexander the Great's father. It is mostly by those names that the brothers are known to history. Perhaps they thought this renaming would mark the two of them as people who were willing to deal with their English neighbors as friends and equals.

But it was not to be. All the tensions between the two groups Weetamoo saw in her childhood only got worse. The English colonists increased greatly in number, and grew more and more suspicious of most of the Native Indian tribes who surrounded them, especially of groups such as the Wampanoag who had strong leaders like Wamsutta/Alexander. The colonists also became more demanding and bossy, treating the Native people like savage children who needed discipline.

During the summer of 1662, Plimoth authorities became alarmed by rumors that Wamsutta was making secret alliances with the powerful Narragansett tribe of Rhode Island, as well as selling land to their rival English colonists there. They demanded that he come into Plimoth for questioning, but he ignored the summons. In July, ten fully armed men from Plimoth surprised Wamsutta, Weetamoo, and a number of their family and friends in a hunting camp near present-day Halifax, Massachusetts. They ordered Wamsutta to come with them, and told him "if he stir'd or refused to go, he was a dead man."

Wamsutta and some of his party — we do not know if Weetamoo was among them — were force-marched toward Plimoth. In a nearby town, he was interrogated and released, but the healthy young man became desperately ill and died very suddenly on his way home along the Taunton River. He is said to be buried somewhere along the riverbank. The English colonists themselves claimed Wamsutta had such a hot temper that his sheer anger at being captured brought on his fatal illness. But most of the Native people of New England, including his brother Metacom, believed that the English had poisoned Wamsutta in order to do away with a strong leader.

Metacom/Philip succeeded his brother as sachem. Probably the widowed young Weetamoo moved back to live among her Pocassets. We know almost nothing about her for the next thirteen years. She married a third husband, named Quequequananachet, at some point, and later wed another man called Petononowit, who was especially friendly with the English. We don't know whether Weetamoo had children by either her third or fourth husbands, but she is believed to have had at least one child with Wamsutta.

We hear again of Weetamoo in 1675, when it became clear that the Native people and the English were on the brink of war. Metacom said bitterly in a speech to a peace council the colonists called in Rhode Island that only "a small part of the dominion of my ancestors remains. I am determined not to live until I have no country." He did not want to live his life out seeing all his people's lands transferred to white hands and made into fields and fenced pastures.

Metacom's young warriors began holding war dances. But many of the New England Native Americans were divided over whether war with the English would be a wise course. Weetamoo and Awashonks were two leaders who were uncertain about what to do, and said so to Captain Benjamin Church, a capable colonial military leader who came to sound them out. Awashonks and Church were fast friends, and she ultimately threw in her lot with the English. Weetamoo told Church that a number of her own young warriors had been attending Metacom's war dances "against her will . . . and she much feared there would be war." She undoubtedly felt strong ties to Metacom, but worried about how devastating a war would be for her Pocassets. Meanwhile, Weetamoo's husband Petononowit was urging her to side with the English.

War finally broke out on June 24, 1675, near Weetamoo's

seaside village of Mettapoiset, when a twenty-year-old English colonist killed a Native man he'd surprised raiding an English house. The next day, some of Metacom's young warriors killed seven colonists, and the war that had been waiting to happen was on, set off by youngsters on both sides.

The colonists quickly mustered a small militia and began pursuing Metacom and his Pokanokets. Unlike the English, Native warriors mostly traveled with their entire families, so the English were chasing after elders, women, and children as well as fighting men. Metacom and his people fled down the peninsula toward his stronghold at Montaup, but when the English got there, they found only abandoned wetu frames and the cooling ashes of campfires. It soon became plain that Metacom had ferried his people by dugouts across Narragansett Bay to Weetamoo's Pocasset country.

Weetamoo had apparently decided that her heart lay with her brother-in-law, and she helped hide both his and her people in the Pocasset swamplands. The English army surrounded them, but Weetamoo managed to sneak every man, woman, and child out of the swamps right under the noses of the soldiers. Throughout the war, Weetamoo would become famous for her ability to maneuver large numbers of her people out of tight situations and into safe retreats.

Weetamoo and her people eventually made their way to shelter in Narragansett country in Rhode Island. According to custom, Wampanoag women were free to marry or divorce as they wished, and she had left behind her English-loving husband Petononowit. Weetamoo next married a Narragansett named Quinnapin, the son of a Narragansett sachem and a handsome warrior in his own right, who joined her and Metacom in the war. This seems to have been a happy marriage.

Though King Philip's War (as it was called) lasted only about a year and a half, it is reckoned by historians as the most deadly of all American wars, considering proportionally the numbers of people on both sides who died in it. More deaths per 100,000 population occurred in this war than in either the American Revolution, the Civil War, or World War II. More than half of the ninety or so English settlements in Massachusetts and Rhode Island were attacked, and a good many of them were completely burned to the ground. Though this war is seldom taught in school history books, it set the tone for bitter Native American–EuroAmerican relations for the next two hundred years and more.

Weetamoo is not easy to track during most of the war, partly because the people who wrote firsthand about battles were almost all English men who did not pay much attention to women warriors. There are two exceptions. One is Benjamin Church, the colonial military leader who seems to have had greater knowledge than most English of the Native people he fought. He called Weetamoo "next after Philip in the making of the war." The other exception is a remarkable Englishwoman named Mary Rowlandson.

Rowlandson was captured in a raid on the town of Lancaster, Massachusetts, on February 10, 1676, and became the hostage of Quinnapin and Weetamoo. From February until May, when she was ransomed and returned to her family, she was on the run with her captors through Massachusetts and New Hampshire. She recorded her experiences in her 1682 book, *The Narrative of the Captivity and Restoration of Mrs. Mary Rowlandson,* which would remain an American best-seller for many generations. Rowlandson's account is understandably prejudiced, for she lost a baby daughter and other friends and relatives to the attack. But over the months of her captivity she recovers from her grief, and comes to genuinely like both Metacom and Weetamoo's Narragansett husband Quinnapin. She despises Weetamoo, but she has given us the fullest portrait we have of her as a grown woman:

A severe and proud dame was she, bestowing every day in dressing herself neat as much time as any gentry of the land . . . When she had dressed herself, her work was to make wampum and beads.

Rowlandson, of course, had no idea that Weetamoo was a sachem in her own right. She thought Weetamoo was just a bossy person who didn't act modestly, as she believed women should, even though Rowlandson herself was very feisty.

In her account of her captivity, Rowlandson describes the death of Weetamoo's baby, and how other Indians came from afar to "mourn and howl" with Weetamoo and Quinnapin in their grief. She also describes how Weetamoo would snatch the Bible from her when she caught her reading it and toss it out the opening of the wetu.

In early May of 1676, shortly before Mrs. Rowlandson was returned to her family, she describes Weetamoo getting dressed up for a big ceremony:

She had a kersey [linen] coat and was covered with girdles of wampum from the loins upward; her arms from her elbows to her hands were covered with bracelets; there were handfuls of necklaces about her neck; and several sorts of jewels in her ears. She had fine red stockings, and white shoes, her hair powdered and face painted red that was always before black.

It is ironic that these two enemies should both be known for their skill with needle and cloth. Weetamoo loved to do elaborate beadwork, and Rowlandson found favor with her captors because she was deft at sewing caps and shirts. In another time, another place, the two might well have been friends, or at least friendly rivals.

In May of 1676, shortly after Rowlandson was returned to her family, the great blow came to the Indian forces at Peskeompskut. In the early morning of May 19, the English surprised a fishing-camp made up largely of women, children, and elderly people and fired upon them as they slept. The people were already exhausted from life on the run. Their food supplies were running short. It was too early to gather berries and nuts, and they had not had a chance to plant new crops. But this wholesale slaughter of the elders who were their past, the women who carried the seeds of their continuance, and the children who were their future took the spine out of their war-making.

In August of that same summer, Weetamoo attempted to flee back to her home country of southeastern Massachusetts. On August 6, 1676, while she attempted to cross a river clinging to a raft, she drowned in a swift tidal current. The English found her naked body washed up on shore near her childhood home of Mettapoiset. The colonists cut off her head, as was the European custom when dealing with dead enemies, and displayed it on a pole in Taunton, Massachusetts. Many Indian prisoners of war were already being held there, and it is said they cried dreadfully at the sight of the dead and mutilated woman leader whom they loved.

Metacom/Philip was shot shortly thereafter. He was cut into pieces; one hand was given to the governor of Plimoth as a souvenir, and the other was kept by the executioner. His severed head remained skewered on a pole in Plimoth for twenty-five years. Quinnapin was also captured and eventually executed. If Quinnapin and Weetamoo left living children, there is no record of them.

Wootonekanuske and her nine-year-old son were taken prisoner on August 1, 1676. For a while there was much debate among the colonists about whether to execute Philip's wife and child or to sell them into slavery in the Caribbean, as happened to many captives in this war. In fact, most of those captives probably never made it to the Caribbean Islands, where European colonists had become wary of slave revolts. Many of the Indians who were to be sold as slaves were actually marooned on empty islands, or else dumped overboard and drowned at sea.

Finally the authorities agreed to sell Wootonekanuske and her son into slavery. In March of 1677, they were shipped off from Plimoth, supposedly bound for a life of slavery in the West Indies. Their fate is uncertain, but the proud spirits of Wamsutta and Metacom, Wootonekanuske and Weetamoo, live on in the present-day Wampanoag people of southeastern Massachusetts and Rhode Island.

HISTORICAL NOTE

When the Pilgrims came to the shores of Massachusetts, "Place of Big Hills," in December of 1620, they were far from the first European arrivals. The land that would come to be called New England had been visited earlier by Norwegian Vikings, and by fishermen and traders from various countries. These Europeans passed on diseases against which the Native people had no immunity, and many of the local tribes along the coastline suffered epidemics of smallpox and measles. Most of the survivors fled inland. When the Pilgrims landed, they explored a coast where they found abandoned villages and pits where the Indians had stored up corn for the spring planting. The English newcomers helped themselves to the dried corn they found there, seeds that enabled them to survive.

The Pilgrims were astonished when, in time, a few

Native people came forth from villages farther inland and not only greeted them in a friendly manner, but spoke in English. The first visitor, Samoset, was an Abnaki who had learned a little English from the coastal traders in Maine. He soon brought to them Squanto, a Patuxet who had lived a remarkable life.

Years before, Squanto had been captured and taken to England by a British trader. He remained there from 1605 to 1614 and learned to speak English. Soon after he returned to his home, he and about twenty other Indians were kidnapped by another British ship and sold in Spain as slaves. Catholic friars rescued Squanto from captivity and attempted to convert him to Christianity. He made his way back to England, where he lived for a time with a rich merchant and eventually headed for home on a ship voyaging to explore the New England coast. When the captain dropped him off at Patuxet, his home village, he discovered that his people had been swept away in an epidemic, probably the smallpox. Squanto went to live with Massasoit's Pokanoket. About six months later, the Pilgrims settled at Patuxet and called it Plimoth.

Squanto seems to have been unhappy among Massasoit's people. Perhaps he already felt caught and confused between the two worlds, English and Native, where he had dwelled. In any case, when the Pilgrims arrived, he chose to make his home among them. Without the Wampanoags' knowledge of local agriculture, weather patterns, and terrain, and Squanto's services as a translator, the little band of Pilgrims would almost certainly not have made it through their first year.

Another Native who lived with the Pilgrims was Hobbamock, who seems to have been something like Massasoit's resident ambassador to the colony. He kept Massasoit informed about what was going on among them.

And then of course there was Massasoit himself, Ousamequin, or Yellow Feather, the Great Chief, who was largely acknowledged as the Supreme Sachem among all the Wampanoag Nation. Most of them listened to him and followed his advice. In January of 1621, Massasoit marched through the gates of Plimoth with twenty or so of his councilmen, who agreed to lay aside their arms. He and John Carver, the first Plimoth governor, signed a pact that vowed peace and mutual respect. That pact was renewed periodically with William Bradford, Carver's successor, and was more or less kept until Massasoit's death some forty years later.

When the Wampanoags and the Pilgrims first met

in 1620, Indians far outnumbered the Europeans. The English colony consisted of little more than a hundred people, and nearly half of them died of disease and malnutrition that first winter. People on both sides were mostly inclined to cooperate and trade with one another.

But by the time Weetamoo, Wamsutta, and Metacom were in their teens, things had changed radically. English colonists kept settling in New England, taking up more and more space, and the old trade agreements were not working anymore. Wampum and beaver pelts were ceasing to be desirable trade items that gave the Wampanoag an edge in the economy. The Indians could see how their land was ever more rapidly being bought and sneaked and stolen away, and their crops and deer-hunting and clamming-places trampled upon by free-grazing English cattle and pigs. The wise elders on both sides who had been fairly good at keeping the peace and extending courtesy to one another were dying, one by one. A harsher age was coming to southern New England, the age in which Weetamoo and her friends and the second generation of English colonists would grow up.

From the late 1620s onward, more English people emigrated to Massachusetts Bay Colony, to the north of Plimoth. The Puritans of that settlement were more numerous and more religiously strict than the Pilgrims of Plimoth. Their growing presence put more and more pressure on the Wampanoags as they encroached on Native lands and ways of life.

In Weetamoo's younger years, it was a great dilemma to many Indian people about how much of European culture they should accept. Metal goods, especially firearms and copper kettles, and even linen cloth and glass beads, all had their attractions. So did the Coat-men's marks-on-paper. Some Native people were eager to become literate in the Coat-man way, though the English insisted that learning to read and write meant the pupil must convert to Christianity. In the middle 1650s, the Reverend John Eliot started a special school to educate Indians at Harvard University, which accepted a handful of young Native men. This school did not last long, in part because the Indian students grew ill when confined within the dank brick buildings, but it did produce a few graduates. At Harvard today, a plaque marks the school's site where Caleb Cheeshatanmuck, an Aquinnah Wampanoag, graduated in 1665.

Some Native children also attended grammar schools in Cambridge. When he became sachem, Metacom would employ as his secretary an English-speaking Indian named

John Sassamon, a former school teacher, to help him correspond with Plimoth authorities. As an adult, Weetamoo must have had similar help, for there is on record at least one letter sent to her by Plimoth governor Josiah Winslow urging her not to join Metacom/Philip in warfare against the colonists. Neither sachem seems to have become literate in the Coat-man way, though Philip's signature on official papers was a bold P.

Many Native people did turn to Christianity in these years, especially those whose people had been nearly wiped out by epidemics, and who had lost faith in powwaws. In 1650, Reverend John Eliot founded a so-called Praying Town at Natick, in effect a village set aside for Christian Indians where they were to be taught to live and farm in the European fashion. Other Praying Towns were soon established.

On the other hand, many Europeans found themselves deeply drawn to the Native way of life. A century later, inventor and diplomat Benjamin Franklin would say that one real problem for the colonies was the fact that so many children and women who had been captured by Indians did not want to return to life in colonial villages and their white families. They found Indian life marked by generosity, freedom, and wisdom.

During Weetamoo's adolescence, both Indians and

Europeans were strongly influencing each other's culture. It is a great American tragedy that the children of the same people who could share a friendly meal of thanksgiving in the autumn of 1621 would be locked in a terrible war by 1675.

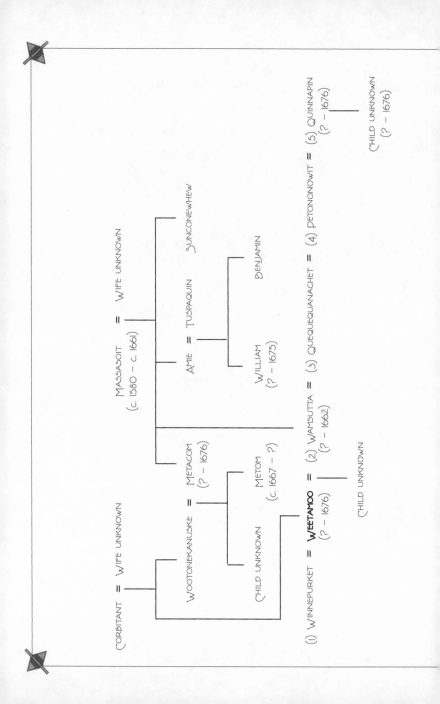

WEETAMOO'S FAMILY TREE

Wampanoag women were free to marry, divorce, and remarry as they wished. Accordingly, Weetamoo was married to five men during her lifetime, three of whom died during their time together.

Men in southern New England tribes were allowed to have more than one wife at a time, though many chose not to. It is not known just how many wives Weetamoo's father, Corbitant, had in his lifetime. However, historical records indicate that Massasoit and his sons Wamsutta and Metacom were all apparently content with a single wife. But when Weetamoo took Quinnapin, the Narragansett sachem and warrior, to be her fifth husband, she joined two wives already established in his household.

The family tree chart portrays the link between Weetamoo's family and that of her husband Wamsutta. We are uncertain of many names and dates in the chart, especially of women. Though women held high status in Wampanoag society, the English historians seldom bothered to record Native American women's names on deeds. Therefore, dates of births and deaths are noted when available. Double lines represent marriages; single lines indicate parentage.

ELDERS

CORBITANT: Father of Weetamoo and Wootonekanuske, he was sachem of the Pocasset band of Wampanoags. Corbitant distrusted the English newcomers and disagreed with Massasoit's policy of being friendly to them. The name(s) of his spouse(s) and dates of his birth and death are unknown.

MASSASOIT: Born around 1580, he was father to at least four children: Wamsutta, Metacom, Amie, and Sunconewhew. Massasoit's real name was Ousamequin, or "Yellow Feather." Sachem of the Pokanoket band of the Wampanoag, he was widely accorded respect from other Wampanoag bands. He was the "chief" with whom the Pilgrims mainly dealt during the first forty years of Plimoth Colony. After his death in 1661, he was succeeded by his son, Wamsutta (Alexander).

CHILDREN OF CORBITANT

WEETAMOO: Corbitant's eldest child and sachem of the Pocassets after her father's death. She had five husbands and was a spiritual and military leader of the Algonquin uprising against the English colonists from 1675 to 1676. She died from drowning on August 6, 1676, while fleeing the English.

WOOTONEKANUSKE: Younger daughter of Corbitant, she married Metacom and together they had one surviving son. She endured King Philip's War, and after the war she and her son were sold into slavery in 1677.

WEETAMOO'S HUSBANDS

WINNEPURKET: Her first husband, the sachem of Saugus, Massachusetts. He died shortly after he and Weetamoo were married.

WAMSUTTA: Her second husband, the sachem of Pokanoket. It is speculated that he and Weetamoo had a child together, but the name and birthdate are unknown. In 1662, he died after being forcibly questioned by hostile English colonists.

QUEQUEQUANACHET: Little is known of Weetamoo's third husband.

PETONONOWIT: Her fourth husband, a Wampanoag who sided with the English colonists. Weetamoo left their marriage at the start of King Philip's War.

QUINNAPIN: Her fifth husband, the grandson of the powerful Narragansett sachem Canonicus and a respected sachem and military leader. He was executed at the close of King Philip's

War; he and Weetamoo had at least one child, who died in the spring of 1676.

CHILDREN OF MASSASOIT

WAMSUTTA: Massasoit's first child, born in the early 1600s, also known as Alexander. He was married to Weetamoo.

METACOM: Also known as King Philip, he was the second son of Massasoit. He succeeded his brother Wamsutta as sachem. He married Weetamoo's younger sister, Wootonekanuske, and it is speculated they had one child who died in infancy as well as a son, possibly named Metom, in 1667. In 1677, this son and Wootonekanuske were sold into slavery.

AMIE: Massasoit's third child and first daughter. She married a sachem named Tuspaquin. Together they had at least two children. One son, William, died in 1675, and the other son, Benjamin, is said to have begun a number of Wampanoag families that claim descent from Massasoit through him.

SUNCONEWHEW: Massasoit's fourth child and third son.

Because no image of Weetamoo exists from her time, Native American Abnaki artist Chris Charleboif drew this picture of the great sachem as he imagined her as a young woman.

An oil painting of the sachem Metacom, Weetamoo's brother-in-law, who became known as King Philip.

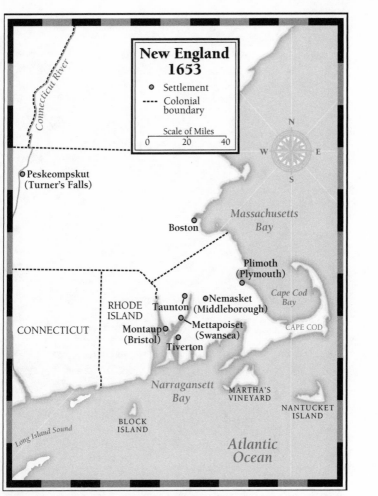

Map of southern New England, circa 1653. Peskeompskut, now Turner's Falls, Massachusetts, was the site of the great massacre of Indians by the English during King Philip's War.

An authentic deed recorded on November 29, 1652, wherein Massasoit and his son Wamsutta sold a tract of land to William Bradford, Captain Standish, John Cooke, and their associates in exchange for yards of cloth, blankets, kettles, and an iron pot, among other commodities. The document is signed at the bottom with Wamsutta's mark.

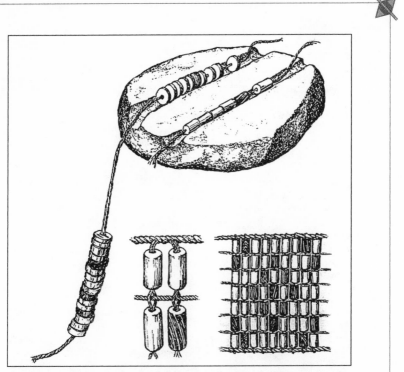

Drawings of wampum made from shells. Strings of wampum were used in making decorative clothing and in trading with the English settlers. In the early years of Plimoth Colony, both Native and English people used these as their form of currency.

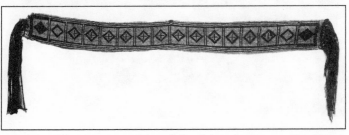

It is believed that this wampum belt might have belonged to Metacom, King Philip.

RAW CRANBERRY RELISH

Ingredients:
4 cups raw cranberries
1 ¼ cups sugar
2 seeded, unpeeled oranges, finely chopped

Wash and pick the stems from the cranberries. Chop cranberries finely, then mix with the sugar and finely chopped oranges.

Store in a covered bowl in the refrigerator and allow to ripen for at least one day, stirring occasionally. Delicious straight from the bowl, or as a relish to serve with turkey or any roasted meat.

Originally, the Native peoples of coastal southern New England did not use oranges or sugar, even the maple sugar beloved by nearby inland tribes. But by the 1650s, they had come to enjoy sweetening. Today Wampanoag and other New Englanders often make this version of the old cranberry dish.

Photograph of wetus, *the typical lodging of the Wampanoag. The bare frames show the structures before bark or reed mat coverings are applied.*

Modern photograph of a Pilgrim's house and outdoor garden as re-created at Plimoth Plantation in Massachusetts. The costume of the Pilgrim woman depicts the authentic dress worn by the English settlers in seventeenth-century New England.

Top left: Photograph of a fiddlehead fern.
Top right: Illustration of the bloodroot plant. The juice of the bloodroot plant was mainly used as an insect repellent or for face painting.

Venison was an important food source for the Wampanoag, and thus the deer hunt was essential. This drawing depicts the ritual of driving the deer into an inescapable V-shaped barrier into the hands of the waiting hunters.

A full view of Hand Rock, which still stands today in a woodsy area of Middleborough, Massachusetts.

Close-up photograph of the rock, with the handprint visible. No one knows who made the handprint, but to some it is representative of someone saying, "I was once here."

GLOSSARY OF CHARACTERS, NATIONS AND TRIBES, PLACES, BEINGS, AND OBJECTS

*indicates fictional characters; (W) indicates a Wampanoag word.

A

Abnaki: An Algonquin-speaking nation located mainly in northwestern New England and upstate New York.

Algonquin: The largest Native language group in North America, extending through Canada, down the Atlantic Seaboard to the Carolinas, and ranging west past the Great Lakes to Montana and southward as far as Oklahoma. The Wampanoag of southern New England are one linguistic and cultural subgroup of the Eastern Algonquin.

Amie: Daughter of Massasoit (Ousamequin), sister of Wamsutta and Metacom.

Aque'ne: Peace (W).

Askutasquash: Squash, gourd, or pumpkin (W).
Attuck: Deer (W).

B

Bittersweet: A vine bearing bright red berries with golden hulls in the autumn. Bittersweet grows thickly in New England swamps.

Blackflies: Tiny insects that swarm and sting during late spring and early summer in New England.

Bloodroot: Spring-blooming members of the poppy family whose stem oozes a thick red-orange juice; used by the Algonquins as a dye, a face-paint, and an insect repellent.

Bradford, William: Off and on, the governor of Plimoth from 1621 until 1657.

C

Carver, John: The first governor of Plimoth, who served from the *Mayflower*'s landing in 1620 until his sudden death in 1621.

Cedar*: Weetamoo's friend, based on the historical person Awashonks, sachem of the Sakonnet band of the Wampanoag nation located around present-day Tiverton, Rhode Island.

Coat-men: Translation of Wautaconuoag (W), the Wampanoag word for the English colonists.

Corbitant: Weetamoo's father, sachem of the Pocassets.

D

Devil's Bridge: A series of submerged rocks and reefs extending from the island of Martha's Vineyard, Massachusetts, eastward toward Nantucket, a stretch long known as hazardous territory by sailors.

E

Eliot, John: The Puritan minister who attempted to convert Native people in southern New England.

G

Glouskabi, Glous'gap: Trickster, hero, and divine Being for many Northeastern Algonquin tribes. He seems to share a number of characteristics with the Maushop Being of more southerly New England Algonquian tribes like Weetamoo's.

Gray Wolf*: Abnaki storyteller who visits at midwinter from his home to the north.

Ground nut: A potato-like plant of moist woodlands whose tubers may be boiled and then roasted for a nutritious meal. One of many plants the Wampanoags introduced to the English.

Gull Girl*: White Frost's daughter; Weetamoo's little cousin.

H

Honckock: Geese (W).

Hubbub: A gambling game in which bones painted half black are tossed in a basket, and players bet on how many of the bones will turn black side up (W).

K

King Philip: The name the English bestowed on Metacom.

King Philip's War: The Algonquin Native revolt of 1675 to 1676 against the English colonists.

Kutchimmoke: Be of good cheer (W).

L

Loon Woman*: Mother of Tall Pine.

Lowatanassik: Midwinter (W); early January.

M

Manitou: Great Spirit; God (W).

Massasoit: "Supreme Sachem," also known as Ousamequin, "Yellow Feather." The main leader of the Wampanoag peoples when the Pilgrims arrived in 1620. He continued to govern until his death in 1661, when Wamsutta, his eldest son, assumed the post. Father of Wamsutta, Metacom, Amie, and Sunconewhew. Best known as the neighboring sachem who diplomatically extended friendship and help to the English colonists at Plimoth.

Maushop: The giant Being who is said to have created much of the land and weather around coastal Massachusetts; husband of Squant.

Metacom: Also known as Philip, the younger son of Massasoit, who grew up to lead Wampanoags and other native people in the rebellion called King Philip's War (1675 to 1676).

Mettapoiset: Present-day Swansea, Massachusetts; Weetamoo's seaside town in her childhood.

Micheenee Keeswush: Late August, early September; "Time of Everlasting Flies" (W).

Montaup: Stronghold of the Pokanokets, Massasoit's people, near present-day Bristol, Rhode Island. It is today the site of Brown University's Haffenreffer Museum, whose collections include many artifacts concerning Wampanoag history. The English always called it Mount Hope.

Munna'mock: Grandmother Moon (W).

N

Nahom: Turkeys (W).

Namassack Keeswush: Time of Catching Fish; late March, early April (W).

Nantucket: Far-Off-Among-Waves (W); island off the coast of Massachusetts, lying east of the larger island of Martha's Vineyard.

Natick: Northeastern Massachusetts inland settlement founded as a "Praying Town" for Christianized Indians.

Neepunna Keeswosh: Moon When Corn Is Ripe; late August, early September (W).

Nemasket: Present-day Middleborough, Massachusetts, about fifteen miles inland from Plymouth Colony.

Nock: To fit an arrow to a bowstring in preparation for shooting.

Nokake: Parched and ground-up corn, an easily packed food that sustained Wampanoag people on long journeys (W).

Noowantamore: I am sorry for you (W).

Nou'gou'mis*: Grandmother (W); here, the affectionate name everyone calls Cedar's storyteller great-aunt, Willow.

O

Ohhomons: Great horned owl (W).

Ohkuk*: Clay pot (W); the name of Weetamoo's puppy.

P

Papone: Winter (W).

Paponakeeswush: Late January; Winter Month (W).

Patuxet: Little Falls (W); present-day Plymouth, Massachusetts.

Pepewarr: Late October, early November; "White Frost" (W).

Peskeompskut: Exploding Rocks (W); present-day Turner's Falls, Massachusetts, a waterfall on the Connecticut River, site of the massacre of many Algonquins by colonists on May 19, 1676.

Pesuponk: Sweat lodge (W).

Plimoth Plantation: The English colony established on the coast of Massachusetts in 1620.

Pocassets: Weetamoo's band of the Wampanoag tribe, residents of present-day northeastern Rhode Island and southeastern Massachusetts.

Pokanokets: Old name for the Wampanoags, the Native people who figure in all the "First Thanksgiving" stories, based in present-day southeastern Massachusetts and northeastern Rhode Island.

Pokeberry: A tall herb whose young shoots are edible, but whose mature leaves and roots are poisonous. It bears glossy dark berries in autumn, often used for dye by Native people.

Powwaw: Spiritual leader, healer, "medicine man" (W).

Praying Town: Seventeenth-century town in New England set aside by English colonists for Christianized Indians.

Q

Quahog: Hardshell clam found along the New England coast (W).

Quay: Hello (W).

Quinne Keeswush: The Long Moon; late November, early December.

R

Razor clam: A long, thin, slightly curved clam found along the New England coast.

Red Hawk*: The Powwaw or "medicine man" of Weetamoo's tribe, the healer and spiritual authority.

Rockweed: A common seaweed along the New England coast, with float bladders that pop in the heat; the seaweed usually used for clambake pits.

S

Sachem: Leader, chief (W).

Sakonnets: A group of Wampanoag, based around present-day Tiverton, Rhode Island.

Saugus: Wampanoag village north of present-day Boston. The name means "swamp" in Wampanoag.

Seal Boy*: White Frost's son; Weetamoo's little cousin.

Snowbird*: Weetamoo's baby sister.

Snowsnake: A favorite Algonquin winter game, which involves sliding a long stick as far as one can thrust along an icy trough dug in the snow.

Spotted sickness: Probably smallpox, possibly measles. Both were often fatal to the Indians of New England who had no natural immunities to European diseases.

Squant: In Weetamoo's time, the Wampanoag spiritual being who protected girls and women, and the wife of Maushop. Later, she seems to have become one of the "little people," a small being for whom people left gifts in order to keep her from doing mischief.

Squocheekeeswush: When the Sun Has Strength to Thaw (W); late January, early February.

Standish, Myles: The leader of the Plimoth army from 1621 to 1653.

Sunconewhew: Baby brother of Metacom, Wamsutta, and Amie; son of Massasoit.

Sunrise Ocean: English translation of the common Algonquin name for the Atlantic.

T

Tall Pine*: Husband of White Frost, Weetamoo's maternal aunt.

Taquontikeeswush: Harvest Moon; late September, early October (W).

Taubotneanawayean: Thank you (W).

Three Sisters: Corn, beans, and squash, the crops that sustain Weetamoo's people.

V

Venison: Deer meat.

W

Wampanoag: "People of the First Light"; Eastern Algonquin people living in southeastern Massachusetts, its off-shore islands, Martha's Vineyard and Nantucket, and eastern Rhode Island.

Wampum: The carved purple and white shells of quahogs, used as trade in seventeenth-century New England (W).

Wamsutta: Oldest son of Massasoit, named Alexander by the English.

Wapicummilcum: When Ice In the River Is Gone; late February, early March.

Wautaconuoag: "Coat-men"; non-native people (W).

Weachamin: Corn (W).

Weetamoo: Daughter of Corbitant, wife of Winnepurket, Wamsutta, Quequequanachet, Petononowit, and Quinnapin; Sachem of the Pocassets, and an ally of her brother-in-law Metacom/Philip in the native revolt called King Philip's War. Her name means "Sweet Heart."

Wequosh: Swans (W).

Wetu: House (W).

White Frost*: Weetamoo's maternal aunt.

Winnepurket: Son of the Sachem of Saugus; Weetamoo's first husband.

Winslow, Josiah: Governor of Plimoth Colony from 1673 to 1680. His father, Edward Winslow, was the man who had the argument with Corbitant about the use of firearms to greet their Native American neighbors.

Wootonekanuske: Weetamoo's younger sister, who grew up to marry Metacom/Philip.

Wuttah: Heart (W).

ABOUT THE NAMES OF THE INDIAN TRIBES AND BANDS

All the Indian people in this story speak some form of Algonquin. Algonquin is the largest Native language group in North America. Speakers of Algonquin languages can be found throughout southern Canada, as far down the eastern seaboard as the Carolinas, west across the Great Lakes and the plains as far as Montana, and southward to Oklahoma. Blackfoot, Cheyenne, Arapaho, Cree, Shawnee, and Anishnabe (Chippewah) are among the many tribes whose languages are Algonquin-based. Algonquin languages are as different from one another as the Latin-based languages of Europe such as French, Spanish, Italian, Roumanian, Portuguese, and Catalán.

One branch of the Algonquin languages is called Eastern Algonquin, spoken by people who lived along the Atlantic coast and slightly inland, all the way from Canada's Maritime Provinces southward through the Carolinas.

A further subdivision of Eastern Algonquin is called Massachusett, spoken by people who lived on the coasts and islands of southeastern New England. Among these Massachusett speakers were the Wampanoag, who included a number of groups like Weetamoo's Pocassets. Within a small area like coastal southern New England, even though people spoke somewhat different dialects, they could generally understand one another.

To the north, in present-day Vermont, New Hampshire, and western New York State, dwelled the Abnaki, who spoke yet another branch of Eastern Algonquin. The fictional character Gray Wolf is one of them. Gray Wolf and the Wampanoags would have shared many words. Since he was a regular trader among the Wampanoags, it would not have been hard for him to learn their speech well enough to be able to tell a story at one of their gatherings.

ABOUT WEETAMOO, SACHEM OF THE POCASSETS

Very little is known about Weetamoo before her adult-hood. She enters history mostly with the events of King Philip's War. Hence, this story is almost entirely fictional, though grounded as solidly as possible in what we do know: the places where her father's Pocassets tended to make their homes; what daily life among the Wampanoag people entailed; and the strains between the Wampanoags and Plimoth Colony.

It is important to emphasize that Weetamoo did not read or write. Though a few girls were apparently accepted into John Eliot's school and boarding homes, only the native boys were apparently taught those skills. Before the Europeans came the native people of New England had their own methods of recording events — drawings painted or etched on rock or birchbark; observations coded into the designs of wampum belts; and, above all, their splendid and complex oral tradition. All over the world, preliterate societies have valued human memory, and gifted storytellers, historians, genealogists, and passers-on of various lore have been treasured in their communities. Today's Wampanoag, though long a literate people, still honor the elders who carry on their oral tradition.

The diary imagines that Weetamoo and her friends are at least curious about "Coat-men's marks-on-paper," though it seems certain none of the historical people in this story learned to read or write beyond being able to make a distinguishing mark, such as the bold P followed by two dots with which Metacom/Philip signed his name to documents.

About the Author

Weetamoo has been a hero of mine for a long time. I'm part Algonquin myself, of Micmac descent on both sides of my family. I grew up hearing tales of King Philip's War, the native rebellion Metacom and Weetamoo led from 1675 to 1676, some twenty years after this story takes place.

Until I was ten, I lived in Northampton, Massachusetts, one of the English towns attacked by the Algonquin forces during the war. Then my family moved to southern Maine, another arena of that conflict. My grandparents often took me on Sunday drives to Peskeompskut, "Exploding Rocks," now called in English Turner's Falls, Massachusetts. Peskeomskut is the site of the May 19, 1676, massacre of Algonquin women, children, and elders by the English colonists, the massacre both Weetamoo and Cedar foresee in this story. My folks made sure I knew what dreadful things happened at that bend of the Connecticut River.

(The great waterfall has been replaced by a hydroelectric dam.)

When I was very young, those same grandparents took me to Montaup, Metacom's stronghold, now the site of Brown University's Haffenreffer Museum in Bristol, Rhode Island. I remember someone hoisting me up to perch in the niche of the rock formation called King Philip's Seat.

Writing about Weetamoo has been important for me. The Native women whom most people in the United States tend to honor are those such as Pocahontas and Sacajawea, who were helpful to the European newcomers. But there were many other brave women like Weetamoo who fought to preserve their own land and culture and gave their lives to that cause.

Few people are aware that a nearly successful Native uprising against the English occurred in the early years of the New England colonies. Even fewer know that one of the leaders of that war was a woman. I was glad of the chance to imagine Weetamoo and her sisters and friends as young people, and think about what would have concerned them in their daily lives. As they grew older, relations between the New England natives and the English became more and more bitter, but it has been fascinating to write about a time when the Wampanoag and their neighbors were still keeping a peace, even if it was an uneasy one.

This is my first book for The Royal Diaries. With my friend and colleague from Laguna Pueblo, Paula Gunn Allen, I've cowritten one other book for Scholastic, *As Long as the Rivers Flow: The Stories of Nine Native Americans,* which was a selection of the Junior Library Guild. My Micmac brother, the native speaker, artist, and storyteller Michael RunningWolf, and I have put together a collection of traditional stories from our own Micmac people, *On the Trail of Elder Brother: Glous'gap Stories of the Micmac Indians* (Persea Books, 2000). Glous'gap is how we Micmac say the name of the hero Glouskabi, who makes an appearance in this book when the Abnaki storyteller Gray Wolf visits Weetamoo's people at midwinter.

Writing this book about Weetamoo brought me strongly back in both body and spirit to the New England of my roots, and what it feels like to be fourteen. One part of the research for this book was rereading my own diaries from when I was that age. In April of 1999, my younger son Caleb and I shared the adventure of hiking powerline cuts through the springtime woods outside Middleborough, Massachusetts — Weetamoo's Nemasket — in our successful search for Hand Rock. If you're ever in that neighborhood, drop me a line, and I'll give you good directions about how to find that Thinking Place!

Acknowledgments

Cover painting by Tim O'Brien

Page 171: Portrait of Weetamoo, by Chris Charleboif.

Page 172: Portrait of King Philip, Haffenreffer Museum of Anthropology, Brown University, Bristol, Rhode Island.

Page 173: Map of southern New England, circa 1653, by Jim McMahon.

Page 174: Deed, November 29, 1652, Mashantucket Pequot Museum and Research Center, Archives & Special Collections: Massasoit (ca. 1590–1661) MSS 19, Mashantucket, Connecticut.

Page 175 (top): Drawing of wampum, from *The New England Indians* by C. Keith Wilbur, page 97, courtesy of Globe Pequot Press, Old Saybrook, Connecticut.

Page 175 (bottom): Wampum belt, Rhode Island Historical Society.

Page 176: Wetus, constructed by the Wampanoag Tribe for the Mashantucket
Pequot Museum and Research Center, Mashantucket Pequot
Museum and Research Center, Mashantucket, Connecticut.

Page 177: Plimoth Plantation re-creation, Superstock, Jacksonville, Florida.

Page 178 (top left): Fiddlehead fern, Superstock, Jacksonville, Florida.

Page 178 (top right): Bloodroot plant, The LuEsther T. Mertz Library of the
New York Botanical Garden, Bronx, New York.

Page 178 (bottom): Deer Hunt, from *The New England Indians* by C. Keith
Wilbur, page 57, courtesy of Globe Pequot Press, Old Saybrook,
Connecticut.

Page 179 (top): Hand Rock, courtesy of Eric Schultz.

Page 179 (bottom): Hand Rock close-up, courtesy of Eric Schultz.

OTHER BOOKS IN THE ROYAL DIARIES SERIES

ELIZABETH I
Red Rose of the House of Tudor
by Kathryn Lasky

CLEOPATRA VII
Daughter of the Nile
by Kristiana Gregory

MARIE ANTOINETTE
Princess of Versailles
by Kathryn Lasky

ISABEL
Jewel of Castilla
by Carolyn Meyer

ANASTASIA
The Last Grand Duchess
by Carolyn Meyer

NZINGHA
Warrior Queen of Matamba
by Patricia C. McKissack

KAIULANI
The People's Princess
by Ellen Emerson White

DEDICATION

I dedicate this book to my beloved part-Algonquin mother, Rita Dunn Clark, who died bravely in the course of its writing, and to Joe Bruchac, the real-life Abnaki story-teller and cultural historian. Thanks, Mom and Joe, two of the great teachers I've been blessed to know in my time.

I thank my husband, John Crawford, for his unfailing support.

Caroline Meyer cheered me through from start to finish, and found on the Internet the phases of the moon in Weetamoo's time.

My brother Mike and his family, Denise, Shaula, and Max Clark, took me on my first trip to Plimoth Plantation, where we watched the wild swans wing over, and the book began to take shape in my head.

My brother Jim is in my heart always, and knows so much of what's in this book.

My son Caleb accompanied me and interpreted maps on that day we poked around the Middleborough woods; my son Josh gave me the quiet retreat of his Seattle house, where I finished Weetamoo's birchbark drawings.

I owe my neighbors John and Judy Mocho: she, for our calming nightly walks and talks; and he, for his techno-rescue of the manuscript.

Michael RunningWolf gave generously of his ongoing wisdom and dial-a-scholar knowledge about colonial firearms and many other topics.

Edith Andrews, also named Weetamoo, of the Aquinnah Wampanoag, has given generously of her wisdom to make this a more accurate account of her ancestors' lives.

Susan Cohen of Writers House is not only the agent of my dreams, but fortunately of my waking life as well.

Sonia Black, your patience and sensitivity through the course of editing this book have sustained me in such great measure.

Wehlalen: Thanks to you all.

Copyright © 2003 by Patricia Clark Smith.

All rights reserved. Published by Scholastic Inc.
SCHOLASTIC, THE ROYAL DIARIES, and associated logos are trademarks
and/or registered trademarks of Scholastic Inc.

No part of this publication may be reproduced, or stored in a retrieval system, or
transmitted in any form or by any means, electronic, mechanical, photocopying,
recording, or otherwise, without written permission of the publisher.
For information regarding permission, write to Scholastic Inc., Attention:
Permissions Department, 557 Broadway, New York, NY 10012.

Library of Congress Cataloging-in-Publication Data
Smith, Patricia Clark.
Weetamoo, heart of the Pocassets / by Patricia Clark Smith.
p. cm. — (The royal diaries)
Summary: The 1653–1654 diary of a fourteen-year-old Pocasset Indian girl, destined
to become a leader of her tribe, describes how her life changes with the seasons,
after a ritual fast she undertakes, and with her tribe's interaction with the English
"Coat-men" of the nearby Plymouth Colony.
ISBN 0-439-12910-9
1. Pocasset Indians. — Juvenile fiction. [1. Pocasset Indians — Fiction. 2. Indians of
North America — Massachusetts — Fiction. 3. Massachusetts — History — New
Plymouth, 1620–1691 — Fiction. 4. Diaries — Fiction] I. Title. II. Series.
PZ7.S65745   We 2001
[Fic] — dc21   00-049243

10 9 8 7 6 5 4 3 2   06 07

The display type was set in P22 Terracotta.
The text type was set in Augereau.
Book design by Elizabeth B. Parisi.
Photo research by Amla Sanghvi.

Printed in the U.S.A. 23
First printing, September 2003